# Undesirable

Devilish #3

## Charity Parkerson

Punk & Sissy Publications

# Copyright

—Warning: This book is intended for readers over the age of 18. Some of my books contain allusions to past abuse and trauma.

# Contents

# Introduction

*FINDING A FATED MATE is an immortal's greatest gift. Unless that mate is Lucifer...literally.*

As a godling, Riku has existed for a long time. He's seen a lot of history and done so alone. He gave up the idea of finding a mate too long ago to remember. When he finally felt that undeniable pull, it came as one hell of a surprise. All the puns intended. He's screwed.

Lucifer shouldn't have a mate. Souls are paired for eternity by his pious sister, and they haven't spoken in several millennia. He's not unhappy with the pairing. Riku is incredibly sexy and everything Lucifer would've chosen for himself. Except Riku doesn't want him, and living apart from the other half of himself is a new level of torture. Sometimes, there are no good answers and his pairing with Riku could literally end the world.

*Undesirable* is the third book in Charity Parkerson's Devilish series where vampires, Weres, demons, gods, and all manner of the supernatural live together beneath the noses of humankind. These books are best when read in order.

# Chapter One

THE CLEAN NIGHT AIR filled Riku's lungs. With his chin turned up to the sky and his eyes closed, all his senses engaged. A smile tugged at the corners of his mouth. He wasn't alone.

Less than a month ago, a red wolf came to town. He was young, alone, angry, frightened, and sad. Riku was all those things too, except for the young part. He was as old as time, but it didn't matter. Riku couldn't die. At least, he didn't think he could. As a godling, he was whatever his god maker had created him to be. Since gods tended to make creatures and toss them aside, no one knew the full extent of his powers. But Riku was full of all the same emotions as Yuri Red.

"Why do you hide?" Riku dropped his chin and stared at the line of trees where Yuri crouched in case Yuri didn't know he spoke to him.

Yuri stepped from behind the trees. He was fully clothed and in human form. Either he had hiked up the mountain on foot or carried his clothes with him.

"How did you know I was there?"

Riku went back to enjoying the bright night sky. Stars twinkled, calling him home to the heavens... where he was no longer welcomed. "I know everything."

He met the young one's whisky-colored stare. "You're here a lot."

A blush tinted his cheeks, making him look even younger. To humans, he probably looked to be in his twenties. He was like most wolves: tall, perfectly formed, and ten times stronger than men. Yuri was the son of an alpha. He was twice as much as most wolves. Yuri was undeniably handsome and a pariah.

"It's peaceful here, and I worry about you. You're always alone."

He was a good person who didn't deserve the bullshit life had handed him. But such was life, and everyone had their battles. "You're alone too. Do you worry about that?"

A bright smile lit Yuri's face, showing his true nature. "I'm not alone. You're here."

Riku laughed. "By your own reasoning, I'm not alone either." He moved to sit by the fire blazing outside his house. It was made from magic and blazed hotter than most. The fire also wouldn't spread or extinguish without Riku's permission. It was his creation. As a cobra living in the mountains, his skin stayed like ice. Maybe he punished himself with the cold. He no longer knew.

"You should be out with people your age, enjoying life. Spending time by the fire with an old man sounds boring." Riku smiled as he said the words. "At least, it would have for me at your age."

Yuri shrugged as he joined Riku, sitting and mimicking his cross-legged pose. "I'm not... I mean, the other wolves." Yuri growled in frustration. It was a very animalistic sound.

Riku nodded. He wouldn't make Yuri explain. Yuri had come to the small town of Wulfe, Washington, from an even smaller town where his father had served as alpha. He was a bit of a refugee. His parents had been rightfully ripped to pieces by the pack for evil deeds. Unfortunately, that hatred spread to Yuri as well. His innocence mattered not at all other than to spare his life. Wulfe's alpha had agreed to take him in. So far, it hadn't gone well.

Riku slapped his knees. "Well, I suppose it's up to me, then. Someone has to make you act your age." He stood. "Let's go."

Yuri stood too, but he looked confused. "Where?"

With an evil smile growing, Riku grabbed Yuri's arm and vanished. They reappeared behind a nightclub. Music thumped. Laughter and chatter filled the air. Riku headed around the building to the front door with Yuri hot on his heels.

"Where are we? What is this place?"

"San Francisco. It's a dance club."

He breezed past security without paying and with Yuri in tow. Riku ensured the bouncer manning the door didn't even notice. Human minds were easy to manipulate. Inside, the thick crowd made it hard to breathe, but Riku didn't care. There was music in the air. He turned and walked backward, dragging Yuri on to the dance floor.

"I don't know how to dance." He shouted the words to be heard over the crowd. It wasn't necessary. They had supernatural hearing.

Riku reminded him of that by speaking normally. "This type of dancing isn't a skill. It's just moving to the music. Plus, no one cares. They can't dance either and you're sexy. They'll enjoy the show no matter what."

Yuri blushed again, but he let Riku talk him into moving with the music. It didn't take long for him to catch on. "I'm surprised you like this, considering you never leave your mountain."

Riku scoffed. "Are you joking? I'm a cobra." He moved his hips seductively. "I love music. It's in my soul."

"You are pretty mesmerizing."

Riku threw his head back and laughed. He was happy for the first time in a long time. Maybe he needed this night every bit as much as Yuri. A tingle ran down his spine. His gaze shot around the club. There he was, sitting at the bar. His light blue gaze almost penetrated the space between them. He never looked away or moved. Each time the crowd parted slightly, that sexy gaze was still on his skin. Riku's dance became for his other half.

They danced to every song without stopping. Yuri laughed all night, making Riku's heart sing. They felt like friends who had known each other forever. When the music suddenly slowed, someone immediately grabbed Yuri like they weren't about to lose their chance.

Riku felt him moving closer. The crowd parted, making a clear path to Riku—like raw power shoved them aside. Even the way he walked was pure lust. Every eye followed him as he closed the gap between them. Riku didn't move. His entire body stayed frozen at just the thought of his mate's hands on his body. Desire poured from every person on the floor as their greedy stares followed his every step in Riku's direction. His beauty was enthralling, but his terrifying vibe kept anyone from stopping him. There wasn't a single person who didn't watch the six-foot-six perfection make his way to Riku. He cast a spell over the room. Temptation was his forte.

Riku's eyes automatically fell closed as their bodies met. They moved to the music. Riku soaked up every second. The smell. The heat. Fuck. He hadn't known there was so much love and desire in all the world before this man had come into his life. His lips kept brushing Riku's temple. Riku wanted to kiss and bite. He wanted to fuck.

Then the song ended, and lips brushed the shell of his ear one last time. "See you soon." He disappeared as if he had never existed, and Yuri was back.

"Holy shit! Who was that? I've never seen anyone so..." Yuri seemed to fight for words. "Beautiful," he finally said, like it wasn't even a good enough description because it wasn't.

"That was my mate."

Yuri's eyes tried popping from his head. "Wow! What is he? I couldn't tell. Obviously, he's one of us, but I've never felt that much power. I thought my ears would pop."

A sad smile touched Riku's lips. Now the questions would come. Yuri would want to know why he hadn't claimed such a sexy blessing. He would want to know why Riku would torment his mate with a half-life. No doubt he would judge the horrible fate he had been handed. It was always something when anyone learned the truth. "He is Lucifer."

"Oh. Is he that bad? The sexy ones usually are."

An unexpected burst of laughter exploded from Riku. He had to swipe at his eyes while he caught his breath. "No. He is actually *the* Lucifer."

Yuri looked thoughtful for a moment. "I guess that makes sense. He would spread lust and temptation everywhere he went. That's kind of the point of him. Still, wow. The gods must think a hell of a lot of you. That's huge."

Riku shook his head. Yuri wasn't like anyone else. Life should have tainted the hell out of him, but it hadn't. Riku wished the same could be said of him.

Lucifer sat by the fire and waited. He felt Riku heading his way. After spending the entire night watching the way Riku moved, he was hungry. Damn, the way Riku's body moved mesmerized him. Lucifer had always been fascinated by his beauty. Riku didn't possess the coloration of the gods. He had long, dark hair that gleamed in the light. His skin had the golden coloration of being too close to the sun, making him look like the human equivalent of someone of Asian descent. But his eyes, wow. They were what really haunted Lucifer. They were amber and perfectly complemented his sharp face. Lucifer was a greedy, greedy bitch. He wanted his mate; except he wasn't Lucifer's mate. Not really, so he was also enraged. A week and two days ago, he had given Riku two weeks to decide. They would claim each other willingly, or Lucifer would decide for them. He was done dancing to Riku's tune. If Riku didn't want him, he needed to say it. Lucifer was used to suffering. But he wasn't accustomed to having hope, and that was worse than the Hell he ruled.

Riku appeared with his new friend in tow. The boy turned wolf and scampered into the woods the moment he spotted Lucifer. An evil smile pulled at Lucifer's lips. He knew who Lucifer was and did the smart thing. That was good. The moment he was gone, Riku moved to join him. He didn't bother sitting. Riku straddled him. His gaze looked every bit as hungry as Lucifer felt. Fuck him. That was why Lucifer couldn't quit him.

"You're here."

Lucifer snorted at the asinine comment. "Where else would I be?"

Riku's mouth lifted in one corner. "Well, you have an entire kingdom of misfit toys to rule."

Lucifer grabbed Riku's ass and hauled him closer. He loved the way their bod–

ies felt together. It was even better when he was inside Riku. "This is more fun."

"I'd hope so. Hell doesn't sound fun."

Lucifer smirked at the comment. "It can be."

With his arms wrapped around Lucifer's neck, he toyed with the ends of Lucifer's hair. Chill bumps skirted across Lucifer's skin. A wicked light entered Riku's eyes. "With you there, I'll bet."

He was in a mood tonight. Those horrible hopes bolstered, making each breath harder to take. He wanted this. Lucifer wasn't used to asking for permission for anything. He wouldn't in this case either, but he needed Riku to want him. Lucifer loathed the idea of never knowing if Riku would've chosen him of his own free will. If he forced Lucifer's hand, Lucifer would act accordingly, but he desperately wanted the mating other pairings received. It was supposed to be beautiful. There was nothing like that in his life. All that was good had been stripped away.

Lucifer motioned with his head toward the woods. "I didn't know you had a hidden desire to be a father."

"Maybe I just needed a partner in crime so I wouldn't feel guilty for letting go for one night."

Lucifer didn't understand why Riku couldn't see that he could offer Riku an eternity of freedom from the chains he gave himself. "You're feeling reckless, huh?" He unfurled his wings. "You'd better hang on." That was all the warning he gave before taking off.

Riku clung to him, laughing against his neck as Lucifer soared through the air at speeds that would kill a mortal. He twisted and flipped, becoming a living roller coaster ride. Riku's happiness and laughter drove him. He saw inside Riku's mind and heart. Riku loved him and wanted this life with him. Lucifer couldn't understand why Riku wouldn't just give in. He got that Riku was a creation of Jörmungandr, and that ridiculous snake had been prophesied to be the destructors of the world. Lucifer knew Riku feared their pairing would be the thing that threw the snake into a tantrum. Personally, Lucifer thought Jörmungandr didn't give two shits about Riku and didn't even remember creating him. That spoiled god had bigger reasons to hate Lucifer. His thoughts darkened. There was nothing standing in their way except Riku. The time had come to choose: this place or him.

Lucifer slowed and gently floated back to the ground. He didn't land by the fire. Lucifer shifted through time and space, landing next to Riku's bed. He didn't release his prize. Riku didn't seem to be in any hurry to let go either. His lips skimmed Lucifer's neck before he nibbled the same spot. Lucifer had to take a deep breath. Patience wasn't a word he knew. Riku sucked the place he had bitten. A moan rose inside Lucifer's throat. He couldn't stop the sound from falling from his lips.

*Don't tease me.* Lucifer sent out the thought. He wanted the connection of being in each other's minds. It fed his darkness, knowing he was so close to owning all of Riku. Riku was every bit as powerful as Lucifer. He just didn't realize it or unleash it.

*I never tease you.*

Satisfaction poured through him as the words brushed his brain. He took Riku down onto the bed, covering Riku's body with his. *That's not the least bit true.* He captured Riku's mouth. Lucifer ran his hand down Riku's body. His clothes disappeared beneath his touch. Lucifer willed his own clothes away too, leaving their nude bodies molded together.

Riku moaned. The sound vibrated through their kiss.

Lucifer didn't put away his wings. They were as long as his body and kept them warm. He was used to the heat of Hell, and Riku was a snake born of the heavens. This world was cold. Lucifer resented the way Riku kept forcing him to come here, where they were equally miserable.

Their bodies moved together, as if seeking more without any need for their minds. It was natural and instinctual for them to be one. They were two halves, fitting together seamlessly. Each created for the other. Being apart was physically painful sometimes. Lucifer always felt Riku missing from him. It was torturous.

Their fingers linked. It wasn't enough. Greediness overwhelmed him. With a single thought, he had Riku lubed and ready to go. It wasn't in his nature to wait or ask. The only pleasure that mattered was his. He shifted positions and impaled Riku. Lucifer felt everything Riku felt. He shifted positions again to get a better angle. Riku's pleasure was his ecstasy. Lucifer had to please himself. He was greedy like that. Lucifer rocked inside Riku, savoring every moment. They didn't speak. There wasn't a need. Plus, Lucifer was overwhelmed. It was like this every time he was with Riku. He hadn't known anything pure before Riku. The idea of them always fucked with his head. He was the fallen one, banished from all things good. Yet he had been given this, and it didn't make sense. The closer he took them toward the edge, the clearer everything became and the darker he turned. Riku made no attempt to bite him. This was a new level of torment. Maybe the gods had gotten bored and devised this new way to punish him. It worked. He was officially being torn to shreds.

*I feel your pain, and it's killing me.*

*Then let's make it stop.* He had to. Lucifer tore his mouth away and did the only thing his sanity could handle. He bit Riku. Blood filled his mouth. He drank, bathing in the euphoria of finally tying his mate to him. Riku would feel him in ways he never had before after this. He belonged to Lucifer. Lucifer owned him and it was pure bliss.

Except Riku didn't do the same. He writhed beneath Lucifer, but he didn't claim him. Rage and hurt built to a level he had never known.

*Bite me.*

Riku gasped for air. He was on the edge. Lucifer felt it.

*Bite me, Riku. Please? I've never begged anyone for anything in my entire existence, but I'm begging you. Claim me. Please?*

The ugly desperation hung between them for a heartbeat as their gazes met. Lucifer knew. Riku would never choose him. The pain made him dangerous. He was like an injured animal ready to tear apart the only thing he loved more than himself. The only thing he loved, period.

"I never thought I could hate you." He vanished and reappeared inside his bedroom in Hell, leaving behind his black heart. A roar tore from him that shook the earth. With his eyes squeezed closed and his fists clenched, he screamed, hoping to make the anger smaller. The walls vibrated and glass shattered. He felt all the demons scrambling for cover. His vision turned red and then black. When he could see again, blood coated his hands and arms. He smelled the copper on his face. As always, he had no clue what he had done. In the end, he was left fighting for air and he was still empty. It was over. They were done. He was done.

# Chapter Two

TEARS STREAKED BACK INTO Riku's hair. He stared at the ceiling, seeing nothing. Lucifer's pain crushed the air from his lungs, making it impossible to breathe. He was tied to Lucifer now. Part of him lived in Hell, tortured in a way he never knew existed. His angel. His baby. Riku wanted to skin himself alive to get away from the burning sensation. He couldn't draw a single breath. Lucifer never gave him time to explain. He always just disappeared, incapable of hearing Riku.

The bed shifted slightly. Yuri was in wolf form and testing the strength of the frame before hopping onto the mattress. He dropped to his belly and crawled. His ears were flat, as if scared of his welcome. Riku held up the blanket, inviting him to share. Yuri snuggled close and licked the tears from Riku's face.

Riku ran his fingers through Yuri's fur. He felt nothing but the howling loss of Lucifer. It was as if he died, leaving Riku alone and suffering. There was no description harsh enough for the sensation of having his soul stitched to Lucifer, only to have it ripped away again to burn in Hell. His sanity was on the brink.

He heard Yuri's breathing deepen. Riku glanced over at the huge sleeping wolf at his side. While he still felt a deep affection for the boy, his pain drowned everything. He couldn't save himself. Riku was done. He slipped from the bed and stepped outside. The fire that always blazed from his magic still danced in the dark. Riku didn't hesitate. He didn't slow. His feet carried him straight into the fire as if they couldn't get to the end fast enough. Nothing happened. Tears streamed down his face, turning to steam as Riku stood in the center of the flames, praying for death to take him. He couldn't die. There would be no peace for him. This was the cruel fate he had been handed, and he had no idea how to deal. He had been ready to leave this existence the moment he had left the bed. That was what he wanted. Now he didn't know what to do. Riku couldn't go on without Lucifer. He couldn't feel like this. The pain was more than he could handle. This was how Lucifer felt all the time and had for more years than anyone could fathom. Riku understood that now. How was he still standing? Why hadn't he destroyed everything? Riku wanted to. He needed everything to burn the way his body refused to do.

A pained howl filled the air.

Riku's gaze shot toward the sound. He didn't have time to react before Yuri launched himself inside the fire, knocking Riku to the ground outside the flames. The scent of burning fur and flesh assailed his senses. Riku sprang into action, putting out the fire that still burned hot on Yuri's thick coat, melting away his skin. Horror raced through him, cutting its way into his pain and making things worse. Yuri wasn't healing the way a Were should. Fuck. It was the magic. His fire wasn't meant to go out. It continued to burn until Riku willed it away. Riku tried to heal him, since his magic had done this. Nothing happened. He snatched Yuri from the ground. The poor wolf didn't make a sound. Shock from the pain had knocked him unconscious. Riku felt the life slipping from him. He disappeared and reappeared on the lawn of the town's healer. Frost Leo had been sent to their town by Goddess Celeste. If anyone could help, it would be him. The moment he landed, alarms blared. Vampires appeared like smoke—weapons drawn and ready.

"Please? He needs Frost."

A red-haired Scottish vamp with a thick accent stepped forward. Riku thought his name was Fen. "I'll take him." He easily plucked Yuri from his arms. Concern etched his features as Yuri came awake with a loud whine and fought for his life before falling limp again. The pain was too great for his system to handle.

Fen ran for the door to the cabin Frost shared with his husband. It flew open a moment before Fen reached it. Frost stood in the doorway. Riku had done all he could. He vanished, returning to his bed. Riku didn't have the strength to do anything else. Pain suffocated him and made his body too heavy to carry. The tears never stopped. He couldn't force them away. Riku was useless now. Broken. Maybe he couldn't die, but he could refuse to live. The gods might have cursed him with this, but they couldn't make him continue on.

He had no idea how much time passed, but light streaked across the sky when the bed dipped again. A burned and half dead wolf crawled into bed with him.

"He wouldn't stop fighting until we brought him back to you." Frost stood by the bed, looking stern and uncertain of his welcome. "I'll have to treat him here."

Riku ran his fingers through Yuri's fur in a spot that was untouched by burns. "Why?" The question came out sounding hoarse. It was the only word he could push past the pain.

*I watched my pack tear my mom to pieces. She didn't deserve it and there was nothing I could do. I wasn't strong enough. You're all I have. I won't watch you die too.*

The words brushed Riku's mind, making him feel less alone. He could hear almost anyone's thoughts anytime he wanted. This was different. Yuri had pushed his words into Riku's head. He was the strength Riku didn't have.

Frost worked on helping Yuri heal his wounds. "How did this happen?"

Riku motioned lifelessly toward the direction of the fire. "The fire." That was all he had. He couldn't do this.

Frost met his stare.

Riku's vision blurred as more tears fell.

Frost's hand lifted. He visibly hesitated before setting it on Riku's arm. He immediately jumped away and bent at the waist, fighting to catch his breath.

Riku realized Frost had tried to take away his pain. He was mostly human, with some druid blood. Frost was a leopard's mate and couldn't die, but he also couldn't endure what Riku could, and even Riku couldn't bear this.

"Don't do that again."

Frost paced away, breathing heavily. Riku heard Frost's mate, mentally panicking and begging Frost to tell him he was okay and what was wrong. No doubt he had felt everything Frost had.

Frost tried reassuring him. He squared his shoulders and went back to helping Yuri. Frost wouldn't look at him. His mind closed to Riku in a way no one had ever accomplished. The move shocked him enough to let him think clearly for a moment. Frost was way more power-ful than Riku had realized. Celeste obvi-ously hadn't told him everything about the healer. His confusion doubled as his touch healed the majority of the mag-ical burns in a way even Riku hadn't been able to do. Unfortunately, not all of Yuri's fur regrew.

He felt Yuri go limp with relief.

Frost gave a sharp nod and headed for the door without looking back. The odd interaction cut through Riku's pain in a way he couldn't explain. It was almost as if Frost was angry with him. That gave him something else to focus on. It gave him the tiniest reason to survive. He clung to the mystery with every ounce he had left. Riku had to hang on to something. Otherwise, he had no idea what he would do. There were hotter fires he could make.

Frost waited until he made it halfway down the mountain before pulling to the side of the road. He climbed from his SUV and took a deep breath. While he had no idea if Lucifer heard, he called to him. He didn't expect him to show. Lucifer was at no one's beck and call. He might do anything. Hell, Frost was probably insane for thinking Lucifer would even hear him.

Lucifer appeared. His eyes were terrifying. Everything about him was an alarm blaring. He was an injured and feral animal.

Frost closed the distance between them and wrapped his arms around him. Riku's pain had nothing on Lucifer's. Frost thought he might die. His sanity felt ripped to shreds. He closed his mind to his mate to save him from this. It took a moment, but Lucifer's arms closed around him. They shared an odd sort of bond. Lucifer had appeared in his life shortly after Frost had come to town. For whatever reason, Frost felt a kinship. He saw something good in him. Lucifer's rage was the mask of pain. It saved him. The anger was all he had.

"He wouldn't..."

Frost nodded against Lucifer's wide chest. "I saw."

"This is a goodbye."

Frost nodded again. "I know."

"Things here are too..."

"I know," Frost repeated. Things were beyond complicated when it came to Lucifer. He had been tortured for too long.

Lucifer was beyond saving. While he had moments of lucidity where he was in control, that wasn't always true. The longer he stayed here, the more danger the world was in. He might do anything and not even recall what he had done. Most of his mind was gone. Riku had filled in the blank spots, shoring him up, but now that was gone. He had been rejected and there was so much hurt and anger on top of what he had already endured. Frost felt it, even though he also felt Lucifer trying to temper it and save Frost.

Frost took a step back. He swiped at the tears that fell he couldn't control. "I'm here. If you need me, just come to me."

A sad smile touched the features of what had to be the most beautiful creature created. That was why he was tortured. One reason, anyhow. The reason that had started it all. Very few beings knew that, and Frost only knew because Lucifer let him see it. The story had been purposely spread of him being jealous of the world and being cast out. It was the very first smear campaign in the universe's existence. The truth was so much worse. So much darker.

A sad smile came and went again. "I really should sue over that fucking bible."

A watery laugh burst from Frost. Even in his pain, Lucifer tried to lessen his impact on Frost by hiding behind humor.

"You're an idiot to cry for me."

"Maybe."

Lucifer tried for a genuine smile. "Don't hate him. I would've rejected me too."

"Sorry. I can't help it right now. You're his mate. There's nothing that would stop me from being with mine. No fear is that big and no act too violent. He's mine. I can't relate to Riku's decision."

Lucifer kissed his cheek. "Go home to your mate. Forget about me. This is just the new way they found to torment me. I don't want you pulled into the game. If they think they can use you to hurt me, they will. Don't think of me again."

He vanished, leaving Frost feeling cold. His gaze moved up the mountain. He could still see the orange glow of the fire that raged outside Riku's place. There was no way Riku didn't know all the same things Frost did about Lucifer. Yet he still wouldn't accept him. He understood it was complicated. Frost got it would likely be hard, but he had been chosen to be with Lucifer. It enraged him to think about anyone rejecting their mate. That was a hell no one deserved, most especially a man who already literally lived in Hell. Frost had never felt more helpless in his life.

*Please stop shutting me out. You're scaring me.*

Frost startled as Gemini's words caressed his mind. He had been so overwhelmed by pain he had lost himself.

*It's okay, baby. I'm okay. I love you.* Goddess, he loved Gemini so much. He was good and pure. The longer Frost spent among the supernatural community, the more he realized how rare that goodness was.

*I love you more. Do I need to come get you?*

A smile tugged at Frost's lips as he climbed inside his SUV. *No, baby. I'm on my way. Will you hold me when I get home?*

*Always. I've got what you need.*

Frost knew he did. He couldn't be more thankful.

Lucifer had learned a long time ago that the key to survival was distraction. If he ever stopped to look at things, he would destroy everything with an ease that terrified even him. Where would he be sent then?

Frost Leo fascinated him. There was something in his blood even Lucifer couldn't read. He felt certain it was some form of magic. It didn't feel natural—more like created. Druids were a secretive bunch. They had the power to hide their doings. Eventually, there were no more mysteries, but Frost was an enigma. Lucifer enjoyed a good puzzle. That was why he stayed glued to him. Plus, he couldn't bring himself to stay away from this ridiculous little town. His mate was here, wanted or not. Still, Lucifer hid. Riku hadn't claimed him. That meant Lucifer still had the ability to cloak himself from his other half. But Lucifer couldn't go anywhere near him. He was no longer in control. Lucifer didn't doubt his ability to kill a godling. He just might. It was easier and more peaceful to stay glued to Frost. He spent the whole day watching him cuddle with his mate. They were what he wanted for himself, even though he could never admit that to anyone. Lucifer's job was to protect this stupid little ball of water from the evil bubbling beneath its surface. He couldn't be soft. Not that he had ever been even before Celeste created this place.

After a day of spooning his mate, Frost headed into the hospital.

Lucifer followed.

Frost had first come to Wulfe as the new ER doctor. It was a dumb job. He was needed in the community. There were plenty of human doctors. Frost was a magical healer. He needed to leave the humans to someone else. Luckily, Lucifer enjoyed mischief as much as he did a mystery. So, Lucifer had meddled. He looked forward to seeing his handiwork.

"What are you doing here?"

The blonde nurse who stopped Frost looked genuinely confused.

Frost's eyebrows drew together. "What do you mean?"

She motioned toward a nearby doctor. "I thought Dr. Diablo had taken your place so you can work home care."

Glory turned at the mention of his name. His gaze slid Lucifer's way before bouncing back to Frost. While no one else could see him, Glory was his creation. He saw through the glamor, keeping Lucifer hidden. "Dr. Leo, I assume."

Frost glanced between the nurse and Glory. "Um. I'm confused."

Thankfully, Glory took control of the situation. "I heard you might come in today to thank me for taking your place."

Lucifer bit back a laugh. Glory was a pride demon. His conceit made him perfect to play doctor.

He watched the truth dawn on Frost. His hospital position had been removed from his plate. Frost had gotten pretty good at rolling with the punches since finding himself the healer of a tiny supernatural community when he hadn't even known any of this existed. This was different, apparently. He wouldn't let this go without questions.

Frost motioned for Glory to join him off to the side for a private conversation. He waited until they were out of earshot. "Okay. Who in the fuck are you and what's happening?"

Glory clutched his clipboard and rocked back on his heels. "I'm Glory Diablo.

I was sent to relieve you of your hospital duties. Apparently, the community needs you more." He made a circular gesture as if searching for the right words. "For whatever reason, you're," Glory swallowed as if tasting something bad, "special."

Lucifer didn't actually give a fuck about the community. He just liked stirring up shit. But watching Glory try to be human when he was so much more powerful than most anyone in this town was funny as fuck.

"Are you even a real doctor?"

Glory snorted. "I'll have you know, I've spent eight centuries as the top medical torture expert in Hell. There's no one more qualified to put people back together. Granted, I only put them back together so I can tear them apart again, but I'm still a skilled professional."

Frost blinked several times. "So you're a..."

"Demon lord," Glory supplied. "Glory Diablo." He repeated his name as if it would mean anything to Frost.

Frost's shoulders expanded on a deep breath. "I see."

Lucifer bit his bottom lip. Frost was hilarious. This was just the distraction he needed.

Glory made a shooing motion. "You can go. An expert is here now."

To his shock, Frost turned and grabbed his arm. He was so surprised, he allowed himself to get towed to the parking lot. A furious-looking Frost spun on him. "What in the fuck did you do?" The words came out in a growl.

Lucifer shrugged. He was comfortable with anger. This was much better than the earlier tears. "You don't need the money and you're running yourself ragged. Gemini deserves better from you than your refusal to let go of this place, so he at least gets some of your time."

Frost's shoulders fell. The fight visibly bled from him. "Is it that bad? Am I ruining my marriage with this whole healer thing?"

Lucifer shrugged. He honestly didn't know, nor did he care. But Frost had been driving himself into the ground, and Lucifer didn't want Frost to be mad at him. It was better to blame Frost's stubbornness. "You told me a few weeks ago you couldn't leave the hospital in a lurch and Gemini is paying the price for that. So I sent Glory. He isn't dangerous, only arrogant... unless I order otherwise. That's an excellent trait in a doctor."

Frost pinched the spot between his eyes. When he dropped his hand, he shifted from foot to foot. Lucifer felt him cave. "Thank you. I guess. Is this why that whole earthquake thing happened a few weeks back? The vampires said it felt like demons broke the veil."

"Yep." Lucifer kept up the cheerful facade, but he really wanted to rub his chest and scream at the top of his lungs.

He was here. Riku was only miles away. Every breath was like fire.

"I thought you said earlier was your goodbye."

Lucifer gave in. He massaged his chest. There was a hole he couldn't fill.

Frost's expression softened. "Would you like me to check on him?" The quietly spoken question nearly broke Lucifer. He had come here for distraction, but Frost's powers were too big. Frost felt Lucifer and Lucifer didn't like it.

He fought the building rage. It was no one's fault. This was just who he was. He needed to get back to Hell before he accidentally leveled this town. "Do what you want." He disappeared and reappeared inside his throne room. Demons scattered at the sight of him. The darkness pulsed around him. He had to find something else. Trying for humor hadn't worked. The torture room it was.

# Chapter Three

RIKU MANAGED TO MOVE from the bed to the chair. The change of scenery was only due to Yuri. Yuri's stomach had growled, forcing Riku to magically create some food for the poor kid. Then Yuri had carried him to the table so he wouldn't eat alone. Riku didn't touch anything. He hadn't eaten in so long, he couldn't recall the taste of food. Riku couldn't die, so it didn't matter.

"It's time to talk about this." Yuri shocked him with the firm tone. He didn't stop there. "I'm not leaving you, but you have to explain things."

That was fair, since Yuri refused to leave. Riku didn't really want him to go. Not because he needed him, but he knew Yuri had nowhere to go. This meal was likely the first he'd had in a while, gauging by the way he devoured everything.

"What do you want to know?" His voice sounded like shit. It hurt to talk.

Yuri shrugged. "What happened? Why did it happen? Everything, I guess." He shoved a piece of steak in his mouth and chewed while he waited for Riku to answer.

Riku didn't have the strength for a long story. "Lucifer is my soulmate. That means I can't go back to heaven. Since he's banished, as his other half, I am too. I'm a creation of Jörmungandr. That means I can't claim him."

Yuri waved his hand. "Wait. Why does that mean you can't claim him?"

Fuck, he was tired. He took a breath. "Jörmungandr is prophesied to be the one who ends the world. It's possible I'm the catalyst. If I claim Lucifer, who is loathed by my maker, it could be what sets in motion the end of everything here. His hatred of Lucifer is why Goddess Celeste had to banish him to Hell. It's a whole thing that no one really talks about. Even I don't know the full story, since it's a heavily guarded secret, but Hell is the only place he's safe. He can't be seen by the gods there. The darkness cloaks everything."

Yuri lowered his voice—like they would be overheard. "Is it terrible there?"

Riku started to say he had no clue, but then he recalled a conversation he had once shared with Lucifer. "I think it must be for the damned, but I think Lucifer has carved out a bit of a utopia for himself there to make it tolerable."

"And you say no one can see what he does there—like at all?" Yuri posed the question, as if needing clarification.

"That's what Celeste says. Not even her."

"So, if no one can see there and he's made a utopia for himself, then why don't you live there with him? You could claim him, and no one would know."

Riku blinked. Months of mental tor-ture and looking at every possibility and Yuri just solved things as if the answer should have been obvious all along. In fact, where in the hell had he expected they would live if and when he claimed him? No pun intended. Lucifer couldn't stay here. They couldn't go to the heav-ens. Lucifer had talked to him about his golden palace and Riku still hadn't clicked any pieces together.

Horror washed over him. Lucifer had begged. He had literally pleaded with Riku. Riku had brought him low, and he felt Lucifer's hatred. Throughout every second, Lucifer had known they would stay safely in Hell. He thought Riku just didn't want him. The pains in his chest doubled. He would have thrown up if there had been anything in his stomach.

Riku needed to get to him. He needed to explain a few things. More stood in the way than simply being seen. They needed to talk, but Lucifer would never forgive him. Holy shit. Lucifer would never forgive him. That one thought kept repeating and getting bigger. He had to be the one to go way beyond halfway. Riku would have to beg twice as hard as Lucifer had, but he couldn't because Lucifer was out of his reach.

Riku focused on Yuri—certain he had all the answers now. "How do you get to Hell?"

Yuri shifted in his seat. He looked uncomfortable. "I don't know. You die after having been a bad person, I guess." His gaze dropped to his plate. "I guess my dad is probably there."

Riku's heart squeezed. Yuri was a mess too and Riku hurt so badly, he didn't know how to help. He felt terrible for being a burden on top of Yuri's problems. "Would you do me a favor?"

Yuri's sweet brown gaze locked on him. "Anything."

"Will you stay here? I need someone to keep this place safe while I'm gone. I'll make sure you have more than enough money to cover everything."

Yuri's face screwed up in confusion. "Sure, but where are you going?"

Riku took a breath. He felt a spark of hope and it became a lifeline he couldn't ignore. "To find my way into Hell."

A knock landed on the door.

Riku felt Frost on the other side. He opened the door with his mind, allowing Frost entry. In fact, he was more than a little excited to see the guy. His timing was perfect.

"Dr. Leo."

Frost looked more than a little confused at the greeting. They were friends. He had never called Frost by anything other than his name. "Is that greeting your way of letting me know we're no longer friends?"

Riku waved him inside. "No...unless you no longer wish to be friends." He genuinely hoped that wasn't the case. "I need your professional services."

Frost stepped inside. His green gaze slid Yuri's way, as if Riku's claim had his concern skyrocketing over Yuri's burns. "Are you okay? Are you in pain today?"

Riku wanted to talk all over their conversation, but Yuri had gotten burned because of him. He needed to know the answer to Frost's questions, since he had been too self-involved to ask.

"I'm fine, other than a few spots. Hopefully, they eventually heal too. Thank you for whatever you did yesterday. I don't know why I couldn't heal on my own. That's never happened."

A sweet smile touched Frost's lips. "You're very welcome. If it helps, I don't know how I heal people. It just kind of happens." Frost looked a little concerned over the admission. He wondered if anyone bothered to talk to him about his growing powers.

Right now, Riku had bigger issues. An unhinged Lucifer was bad for everyone. "I need you to kill me."

Every eye snapped his way. "What?" Both men said the word at different volumes at the same time.

Riku gave him a sharp nod. His mind was set. If dying was how he got into Hell, then he was willing. "Lucifer needs me. Hell is the only place I can be with him, but I'm a godling. If there's a way for me to die, I don't know it. You're an expert on anatomy. So, I need you to kill me."

Frost's mouth opened and closed several times, like a fish out of water.

"No." Yuri sounded broken. "You can't die. I can't handle that. I got burned for you! My fur still hasn't grown back in spots."

Riku reached across the table and took his hand. He squeezed. "No one really dies. If Lucifer can visit me, I can visit you. Everything earthy I own is yours now. But I have to go to my mate. He needs me." Riku swallowed. His voice broke. "And I need him. It's unnatural to live without your other half. I can't do it." He focused on Frost. "Please."

Frost closed the door. "All right, then. Let's figure this out."

The first real spurt of joy hit since all this bullshit began. Frost would help. Riku would find a way to Lucifer, and he would be the one who begged. They would be together even if it killed him. Whoops. He supposed it would.

With his feet braced on the coffee table, Lucifer threw a ball and waited. Brownie brought it back. It was a monotonous game. He was bored, but Brownie was entertained. The sound of the rubber ball hitting the marble floor gave him something to focus on and busy his mind. He couldn't think about anything important. Lucifer refused to think.

Something scurried across the corner of his vision. His head whipped in that direction. A tiny white fox jumped from spot to spot, trying—badly—to stay hidden. He had no idea why Brownie showed no interest in the animal, except maybe because it was no animal. He smelled heaven.

Lucifer drew the scent deep into lungs. It was cotton candy and sunlight. It had been so long. He hated the smell. "You're either very brave or extremely dumb. I'm leaning toward the latter. Show yourself before I make you."

The fox became a tiny guy. Blond hair with blue eyes that mimicked the sky. Angel colors, but he was no angel. He was something else. Something scarily powerful. Lucifer wasn't the most powerful creature in the room any longer. That was why Brownie hadn't reacted.

A small wave greeted him, making him more curious by the second. "Hi."

"Um. Who the fuck are you?"

"Tamil. Everyone calls me Tam, though. I guess you can choose which you pre-fer since you're my... uncle." He said the word slowly as if unsure. "Great uncle. Great, great uncle. I don't know. I'm Ce-leste's great grandson. Micheal Jr. is my dad."

Lucifer recognized the scent of mag-ic now. It was very similar to how Frost smelled, except a billion times more powerful. A nephilim. No... not a nephilim, but a druid shifter angel.

Holy shit. He was a trifecta of power. Lucifer also smelled something else.

"Come here."

Tam twisted his fingers and didn't budge.

Lucifer didn't miss the way he shook. It was obvious he was scared and suffering a huge PTSD episode, but he still stood tall. Fascinating. "I won't harm you." He couldn't if he wanted, but Lucifer never revealed weaknesses.

Tam shuffled closer.

When he was within striking distance, he moved before Tam could jump away. He ran his hand down Tam's arm.

Tam was back across the room in a flash. His gaze darted from side to side, as if watching for an attack, but the shaking had stopped.

Lucifer waited him out.

Tam's expression turned confused. "What did you do to me? I feel better."

"You had demon poison lingering in your blood. I'm the only one who can truly break that curse, since it's my creation. You've been here before."

Tam didn't respond to the accusation. They both knew the only way to get demon sickness was through physical contact with a demon. The only way Tam's had run so deeply... He had been in Lucifer's torture chambers. How had that happened? He had never been more invested.

Tam's gaze was locked on Brownie. "What's that? It looks like a dog, but it's too big."

"It's a hellhound."

A bright smile snapped his way. "No way! He's too cute."

Lucifer fought a smile. He was brave as fuck. "I promise you he is. What did you think hellhounds looked like?"

Tam spread his arms wide. "Huge and bloody. Monsters, I guess. He's adorable. Can I pet him?"

Lucifer cocked his head to one side and studied Tam. A growing suspicion took hold. "You have my permission. His name is Brownie."

Tam flashed him a smile as he dropped to his knees and gave Brownie all the love—much to Brownie's heavenly delight.

"Brownie? You named a hellhound Brownie? I mean, it fits, but doesn't he get teased by all the other dogs?"

Lucifer shook his head. This had been the oddest day. "I'm not fooled, you know? You touch things so you can take their form later."

Tam kept his gaze locked on Brownie. Lucifer knew he was right. That was how shifters worked. They could change into anything their heart desired, but they had to have touched the object first. Tam likely pulled this trick all the time, using the ruse of innocence to get his way. Truthfully, he was fully aware of the extent of his power and Lucifer felt the darkness he hid. Lucifer understood why he pretended. He, too, possessed deceptive beauty. It was a weapon and a curse.

"I touch everything because I love animals. They have a purity no other creature can claim." His gaze met Lucifer's. He looked like a different person. Dangerous. "But yes, I also touch everything because I'll never be a victim again."

There it was—like looking in a mirror.

"How can I help you, Tam?"

Tam gave Brownie a final pat and stood. "I have a message from Celeste."

Instant rage nearly took him out. He hadn't heard a fucking word from his sister in so long, he couldn't recall. Now, here was this kid. "Go on." Even Lucifer heard the beast inside him trying to break free.

"Your mate is currently trying every method possible to kill himself so he can find a way into Hell. He loves you. Celeste says to tell you to, and I'm quoting here, 'stop being a weak-ass bitch and get your man.' She doesn't pair souls out of boredom. It's her job. Riku is truly yours. This isn't some way to fuck you up or anything. He's a gift. If you don't want him, then say so. She'll return Riku to the heavens and set you free."

"How will that set me free? If he's my other half, then that can't be undone. We'll both still be only one half of a whole. She's the fucking expert. All the rest of us are just fucking guessing how this shit works."

Tam shrugged. "I'm just the messenger. It's all too complicated for me, but I can tell you this. I go to see my grandmother all the time and I have a mate. He's sweet and kind and funny." Tam twisted from side to side, smiling like he had completely lost the plot. He finally stopped and held Lucifer's stare. "When I'm with Celeste, the way I feel isn't muted. I know they say I should feel less there, but I don't. There's never a time when I can tolerate the separation. My guess is, even if she takes Riku to heaven, you'll both still suffer. There's no such thing as freedom without your mate. Whatever has you staying away, it can't be as bad as the pain of being apart. I can't imagine... or maybe I can, and that's why I can't stop talking." He pressed his lips together, as if physically forcing himself to stop.

"Riku doesn't want me." The words were like hot coals in his throat. "This isn't me being a weak-ass bitch. He doesn't want me."

Tam's hands rose and fell. "I mean, obviously, he does. Why else would he try to come here?" Tam looked thoughtful. "But I have no idea why he thinks he has to die to get here. Demons and you and me and probably hellhounds and birds." He stared into space again as if lost in his head. Finally, he snapped back to reality. "Why are there so many birds here? It's really out of control." He waved his arms. "My point is that... no, really, I can't take it. Why are there so many birds?"

"They're my spies," he answered absently.

While Tam had obviously totally forgotten his point, Lucifer got it. Creatures crossed the veil unharmed all the time. Riku didn't need to die. Why was he trying to die? Maybe his actions had nothing to do with Lucifer. It was more likely he tried to get out of their mating. Lucifer had claimed him and ruined his life. Only death would set him free. Pain bloomed in his chest. This had nothing to do with him. Riku wouldn't come here. He had been given all the chances and hadn't taken them. They were done. He needed to accept that.

Tam sighed. "I see it's up to me. Sheesh. I have a life too, you know. My mate is waiting for me. He shouldn't have to sit on the back burner over something so stupid. Ugh."

Tam turned back into a fox and disappeared inside Lucifer's bedroom as quickly as he had appeared, leaving Lucifer more confused than before he came. It seemed he had a nephew, though. That was interesting. He had to think about anything other than Riku trying to die. Fuck him. If he wanted to be freed that badly, let him suffer. Lucifer had fucking tried. He was done with that bullshit. It was Riku's turn to burn.

# Chapter Four

THEY HAD TRIED POISON, an overdose of anesthesia, medical suffocation, and a few things Frost flat out refused to take part in. Nothing worked. He didn't even feel sick. It was pointless. Riku just couldn't die. Yuri was beyond horrified at first. After the third failed attempt, he had turned morbidly fascinated, just as Frost had done. They stared at him with equal amounts of awe and pity.

"What if you turned into a cobra and a Werebear ate you?"

Frost shook his head at Yuri's suggestion. "The bear would probably die."

"That's true. Huh. I'm stumped."

Two sets of eyes landed on Riku. He fought the urge to go back to bed and cry some more.

The front door burst open and a tiny blond guy struggled his way inside with a huge mirror.

Frost turned in his seat and then shot to his feet. "Tam! Hey. What are you doing here?" He helped Tam get through the door.

"Hey. Sorry it took me so long." He leaned the mirror against the wall and focused on Riku. Damn. He looked exactly like the archangel Micheal, except much smaller. "After you rejected Lucifer, it seems he let out a roar that shattered a majority of the mirrors in between worlds. It took me a minute to find one that would get you near to where he is. I can control where I go, but I can't control where you land."

Frost blinked his way through Tam's babbling. "You mean you can take a mirror to Hell?"

Tam looked a bit cagey at the question. He shifted from foot to foot. "You can under certain circumstances."

Riku shot to his feet. "Are you serious? I can take the mirrors to get to Lucifer."

Tam rubbed his arm, looking more uncomfortable by the second. "Yeah. I mean, this one time anyhow. But you can't tell anyone, okay? You're not tech–

nically supposed to do this. This is just a very special circumstance." His gaze finally locked on Riku. He turned serious. Riku had no idea who the guy was, but he was powerful. It rolled from him in waves. "Once you step through, you can't come back. The way will be sealed. Your only way home is through Lucifer. Nothing leaves Hell without his permission."

Riku nodded. He didn't care. Riku had to be wherever his other half was. Nothing mattered more.

"What if he won't let you come see me?"

Yuri sounded hurt and looked as if it had finally dawned on him this was really happening.

Riku's heart twisted. "Don't worry, okay? Everything is yours. You'll be okay. I promise."

"I don't care about stuff. Surely you know that. I've never had stuff."

Riku hugged Yuri. He pressed his lips to Yuri's ear, keeping their conversation private. "Occasionally, I get glimpses of the future. Obviously, not mine. I can't truly see you clearly either, but I feel how you'll be so, so happy. Trust me. Okay?"

Yuri squeezed him tighter. "Okay. Try, though. I don't want to lose my only friend. I just found you."

Riku kissed his cheek. "I swear I'll do everything I can to visit. But I have to go, okay?"

Yuri nodded and pushed him toward the mirror. "Go. I saw the way he looked at you. You have to find him."

With a smile, Riku faced Tam. "Thank you. I don't know who you are or why you're doing this, but thank you."

A bright smile met his words. "Of course. He's your mate. Now go claim him." He shoved Riku through the mirror. Riku nearly fell. The guy was deceptively strong. Riku quickly righted himself and looked around. The mirror disappeared, as if it had never been there. Riku swallowed. He had no idea where he was or where to go. It looked like he was in the middle of the woods. Scary woods. On fire. He couldn't place what it was, but everything felt terrifying. The knowledge he couldn't go back truly hit him. He was stuck. If Lucifer refused to hear him or forgive him, then what? This would be his home. At least it was warm.

He transformed into a cobra. Riku felt safer in his true form. His venom and fast strike were his weapons. Riku didn't want to be unarmed. He recalled hearing once that if Heaven was a soft harp playing in the corner and a summer sky, then the underworld was an out of tune electric guitar with amps and a starless night. He couldn't see the sky here, but he got it. The peace was gone. Here, there was nothing but every emotion that had already been crushing him ramped up to a billion. His mate was here, though. That kept him moving.

Riku had no clue where he was headed. He simply followed his nose and tried not to panic. Riku had already learned it was impossible for him to die. He recognized this could be a long eternity of aimlessly wandering. He had to start somewhere. Riku had to get to Lucifer.

The moment Riku pierced the veil, Lucifer felt him. He had claimed Riku. Lucifer felt him every second of the day. He had come. Lucifer couldn't risk he was here for any reason that might put him out of his misery. The despair was all he knew.

He followed Riku, silently flying above him. In snake form, Riku moved fast as hell. Unfortunately, he moved in circles. Lucifer shook his head. He obviously had no plan. The only reason he was safe was Lucifer's presence. If he hadn't come straight to Riku, demons would be ripping him to pieces. Why had he chosen this spot? How had he even gotten here?

Obviously spotting his own tracks after making a full circle, Riku froze and returned to human form. He stood with his hands on his hips. Riku sat on the ground and put his head in his hands.

Lucifer felt his exhaustion and hopelessness. The desperation fed his ugly side. Unfortunately, he loved Riku. That was a miracle he never expected. It hurt his chest to watch Riku suffer.

"Giving up that easily, huh?"

Riku's chin shot up. He eyed his surroundings. "I can't see you."

"Look up."

Riku's gaze flipped up his way. He felt the relief rush through Riku. "My fangs are venomous."

The random comment stumped Lucifer.

Thankfully, Riku didn't leave it at that. "You never give me time to talk to say that. I can't bite you. My fangs are venomous. I don't know what it would do to you."

Lucifer's feet hit the ground. He had thought there was nothing Riku could say to fix things. There was no way he could have seen that one coming. "Baby, I can't die. Literally, nothing can kill me."

Riku made a helpless gesture. "I watched gods die in the great demon wars with massive consequences. If you die, there'll be no one to protect the world from the evil you hold at bay. All of Celeste's creations would be destroyed."

Lucifer had never been more confused. He supposed it was his fault. Riku was right. They rarely just sat and talked, especially not about the consequences of their mating. "Why do you think something as simple as venom could harm me?"

He motioned helplessly. "I'm not just a cobra. I'm a godling. That's not simply venom. This is new territory for me." He rubbed his chest. "If I hurt you, it would kill me."

A smile that felt wicked tugged at his lips. He shuffled closer. "Hurt me, baby. That sounds fun."

Riku rolled his eyes, but Lucifer saw the hint of a smile that tried peeking out.

Lucifer smelled victory. He moved even closer, invading Riku's space. "I'm serious. Do as you please. I love it rough. You should bite me. Let's try it."

"Right here. Right now. You just want me to bite you?"

Lucifer couldn't play games anymore. Riku wouldn't leave this forest if he didn't truly want Lucifer. He was done getting hurt. Lucifer would walk away and leave him to wander aimlessly forever. "Mhmm. Yeah. You should definitely sink those sexy teeth into my skin. I want to feel those venomous fangs."

Riku took a step closer. He held Lucifer's stare as he pushed Lucifer's shirt up his torso. He never broke eye contact. Every breath Lucifer took was harder than the last as the heat flared between them. This part of them had never been a problem. They wanted each other, and Lucifer already knew no one else compared. He knew he could twist Riku around his finger if he would just fucking bite him.

"Do it."

At the demand, Riku focused on his task. Once Riku had Lucifer's shirt pushed to his collarbone, he leaned forward and kissed his chest. Lucifer had to lock his knees. Everything in Hell felt stronger. The lust was crippling. Riku licked the spot he kissed. That was all the warning Lucifer got. Riku struck. His fangs pierced his skin. Lucifer felt the venom hit his bloodstream. It burned and then was quickly forgotten. Riku sucked, taking his blood, and nothing could have prepared him. He felt the invisible strings tying their souls together. Lucifer also came in his jeans like Riku was on his knees, blowing him. Sounds came from him that shocked even him. Riku had been right. They shouldn't have done this here, but he couldn't have known. There had never been anyone to warn him. His insides shook. He had never experienced a harder orgasm. His tongue was in Riku's mouth, and he didn't know how it happened.

*Do you plan to take me home now?*

Riku's thoughts hitting him shocked him. He had never had his mind penetrated without his permission. *Are you sure? I have a bed here.*

Riku pulled away and held his stare. "What are you talking about? My home is with you."

It hit him. His brain was slow on the uptake after having his soul rocked. This was real. It was permanent.

Riku's home was with him. He had condemned himself to Hell... for Lucifer.

Riku shook his head. "No. It's not Hell. There's no such place when we're together. Just our home."

With a single thought, they stood inside Lucifer's bedroom. *Their* bedroom. He got to keep Riku. Lucifer planned to enjoy every second.

# Chapter Five

Riku had never consumed a god's blood. Power coursed through him. He felt so dumb, thinking he could possibly hurt Lucifer with something as simple as his venom. He had just been such a fucking mess since learning he was Lucifer's mate. Everything had felt so damned if he did and damned if he didn't. Their pairing could endanger the world, no matter which way he went. So he spent months wrecking his sanity and hurting this god he loved with every fiber of his being.

Everything looked so simple now. Riku had lived long enough to know how to adapt. All it took was a bit of communication and a change in location. Riku didn't give a fuck where he lived.

"It's warmer here." The laughter in Lucifer's voice had Riku smiling. It was obvious Lucifer stayed in his head, always reading every thought.

With a wave of Lucifer's hand, his clothes disappeared.

"Warm is a nice change."

Lucifer eyed his body in a way that had Riku fully invested. "Good. You should never hide any of this ever again."

"I love you."

Lucifer's chin lifted. His sky-blue eyes glimmered. If he had any thoughts, he kept Riku shut out. As mates, his thoughts were Riku's right, but Lucifer was too powerful. He couldn't force Lucifer to let him in. Sometimes, with Lucifer, it was probably for the best he could hide from Riku. He had a bad feeling Lucifer would hurt his feelings. They had claimed each other. He had his other half. Riku fought the urge to fall into another soul-sucking depression. He had purposely never thought about this part—the part where Lucifer would never love him. Riku was property. Coveted as such. That was all. His throat swelled. He didn't think mates were supposed to feel this way. There weren't supposed to be pieces missing.

Lucifer's mouth touched his and Riku forgot to overthink. Riku was powerful too. He had Lucifer nude with a single thought. Lucifer chuckled against his lips. "That's a first for me."

It was ridiculous how happy it made Riku to be the first at anything. "You'll get used to it."

Riku found himself on his back. Lucifer had thrown him through the air, tossing him on the bed like he was nothing. Riku bounced. His gaze raked the golden beauty he had been blessed with. He was obsessed. No one knew how he had suffered without his other half. He longed and died a little more every day. Now he was here. He had no idea what his life would look like now and he gave no fucks. They were together. He was complete. Lucifer wasn't moving. Riku growled in frustration. He wanted what belonged to him.

Lucifer's irresistible eyes landed on him. They turned black. Even the whites of his eyes disappeared. Fangs appeared. "I don't feel right." Lucifer hit the floor with a loud thud.

Riku scrambled from the bed.

Lucifer was in a full-blown seizure.

Riku jumped on top of him and did his best to keep Lucifer from hurting himself. He didn't know what to do. Riku didn't know anyone here. He didn't know where to go for help. It wasn't like he had a way out of Hell to get someone he knew. He was trapped—helpless.

Finally, Lucifer went still. His eyes were open and still solid black. Even though he didn't seem lucid, Riku still babbled in panic.

"I don't know what to do. Tell me what to do."

"Frost."

The word was weak, but Riku understood. "How? I don't know my way out."

Lucifer weakly tapped the floor. A huge dog-like creature crashed into the room. He looked like a Rottweiler except he was five times the size and twice as fluffy with terrifying teeth.

"Brownie will take you. He'll protect you with his life." Every word sounded like it hurt like hell. "You'll have to bring Gemini. The leopard won't—" Lucifer lost consciousness, sending Riku's panic through the roof.

He shot to his feet and focused on Brownie. "How do we get to Frost?"

"Hold on to my collar."

Riku was more than a little surprised by the deep, almost demonic-sounding voice that came from the hound. He had never heard a Were speak in its true form, but he didn't hesitate to obey.

In a single leap, Brownie was on the bed, dragging Riku with him. With another, they were through a mirror on the ceiling. He spotted Frost inside an examination room with Yuri, inspecting the wounds that hadn't healed. Riku magicked clothes on before they broke the surface, so Frost wouldn't be uncomfortable.

Frost scrambled for cover as Brownie broke through first. "What the fuck? Celeste said—"

Riku followed, killing the words on Frost's lips. "I need you. Well, Lucifer does. We have to go."

*Hi, Riku.*

Riku managed a faint smile for Yuri. "Hey, Yuri."

"Go where? Hell?"

"Whoa. Whoa. Whoa. You're not going to Hell." Gemini shot into the room.

Riku didn't have time for this. "Lucifer told me to bring you too, so you can protect Frost."

"I'll be there as well." Lire, a demon personal guard of the Americas king, stepped through the mirror, carrying a bag. "This is a medical kit from Celeste. You've been called to duty."

"In Hell?" Gemini screeched the words. "No. We did not sign up for this. I have to put my foot down this time."

Riku pinched the spot between his eyes while everyone argued amongst themselves. His mate suffered, and they squabbled. He had never been closer to the edge of snapping. Riku was scared and confused and just fucking terrified. He didn't know what to do.

Yuri watched the various creatures argue while doing his best to stay out of the way. The entire scene made him see how much having a mate ruined lives. All they did was stress and fight among themselves. Yuri had truly only wanted peace when he finally submitted to Waylon, the town's alpha, and tried to fit in. He didn't fit, though. That made him sad and a little angry, but whatever.

*Hey.*

The deep, demonic voice in his head pulled Yuri from watching the drama. A huge beast of some kind sat beside him, looking as tired as he was.

*Hi.*

*What happened to your fur?*

Yuri's shoulders fell. He really must look terrible still. *I jumped into a magic fire to save Riku.*

The beast's head bobbed.

Yuri studied him. He also had fur missing near his throat and a deep scar showed. *How'd you get that scar?*

*Bar fight. They're pretty hardcore in Hell. It was honorable of you to save Riku.*

Yuri felt dumb. *Actually, it was idiotic. Riku can't be harmed by fire. He didn't need me.*

*Did you know that?*

*No.*

Another sharp head bob followed his answer.

Yuri kept talking, and he didn't know why. *Frost has been trying to heal me, but whatever magic was in that fire really messed me up. I hurt my foot.* He lifted his front paw. *It just won't get better.* He tried setting it back on the floor and winced.

The beast turned human.

Yuri forgot to breathe. He was every bit as big and scary as a human. That scar was dangerously close to a major artery. Oddly, he wore a collar.

"Let me see that paw."

Yuri lifted his foot again so his new friend could inspect it. While he did, Yuri studied him. There was a name tag on the collar. Brownie.

*Why do you wear a collar?*

"It's a sign of my position. I'm the personal guardian for the dark one. It is a great honor."

*Does that mean you're not a free Were?*

A scary-looking smile touched Brownie's lips. "I'm not a Were. I'm a hellhound. I wasn't created by Odin. Lucifer is my creator. My only god." He brought Yuri's paw to his mouth and licked.

Yuri couldn't look away as Brownie's tongue slid across the wound. Goosebumps skirted his skin. He was transfixed, and it got a little harder to breathe. His wound healed beneath Brownie's tongue. The shock saved him from humiliating himself.

*Oh, my gosh. How did you do that? Thank you!*

"We have the same fire in Hell. Easily healed by the right person."

"Let's just fucking go! Lucifer might be dying right now, and you won't shut the fuck up and move your feet. Get in the goddamn mirror or I'll make you."

Everyone froze, and all heads turned Riku's way.

Brownie smiled. "He is a worthy mate." He looked Yuri's way and turned back into a hellhound. *Are you coming? While they work, I will groom you. You'll have your fur back by the end of the day.*

Yuri didn't hesitate. He hadn't been groomed since he was a pup. Admittedly, he had very different reasons to want it now, but he would die before he said no. He just hoped he didn't expire from embarrassment, since he had no idea how long he would last under that tongue. It was whatever, though. He would go to Hell for this—literally, and he did so with a smile.

Everything was on fire in a way he had never experienced. His blood boiled inside him, eating away at his organs. He healed repeatedly, but it wasn't enough. The internal attacks didn't stop. If Frost didn't hurry, he would die.

The mirror above him swirled. He had dragged himself into bed and now he regretted it. Lucifer had forgotten exactly where his visitors would land. He didn't have time to move before Frost fell, landing solidly on Lucifer.

Frost scrambled away. "Sorry. I didn't expect to fall from the ceiling."

Before Lucifer could respond, a massive leopard landed on his chest, followed by a familiar demon and then a wolf.

"How many more goddamn people plan to assault me?"

Brownie burst through the mirror, but he was smart enough to aim for the edge of the bed. Riku was next. Lucifer gathered every ounce of his strength and caught him, bracing the blow. "Hey, sexy." Even Lucifer heard how awful and weak he sounded.

"Hey, baby. How are you feeling?"

His strength gave out and his arms fell away. "Terrible. I don't know what happened. It's like... I don't know."

"Jörmungandr's weapon has been activated."

Riku and Lucifer's gaze shot to the demon, Lire.

Lucifer's temper spiked. He couldn't strike out the way he wanted. Not only was Lire a traitor to Hell, but he tried scaring away Lucifer's mate with his lies.

"No one cares about your theories, traitor. Jörmungandr can't see us here. He's powerless in my plane."

Lire's ever-changing eyes focused on Lucifer and turned amber. He was a lust demon. Only his mate would see his true face. Everyone else saw their deepest fantasy. His greatest desire was Riku, so he had Riku's eyes.

"Riku was created for you. He is more than just a godling. He's the perfect silent weapon. Jörmungandr knew you couldn't resist his beauty and wouldn't fear his venom. It seems you should have. It's the poison that kills you now. Once you're dead, your demons will overrun the world and destroy all that Celeste has created. His revenge complete without ever lifting a finger."

Riku covered his mouth, looking horrified. "I did this." The words were whispered and muffled, but Lucifer didn't miss them.

No one gave him time to think.

Frost jumped in. "Celeste sent Lire with a medical kit, but I'm not sure how to fix this. All I can think of is blood. You need powerful blood, but I don't know from who or how much."

Riku immediately switched gears, going from terrified to a soldier in an instant. He had fought in many wars and understood triage on the battlefield. "Why blood? How will that help? Just tell me what to do." He made Lucifer proud. Lucifer just wished this entire thing wouldn't destroy them the way he knew it would. If he lived, Riku would hate him, because now there was no avoiding the truth.

Frost blinked at him, and Lucifer knew—there was no going back. He was about to drop Lucifer's biggest secret. "As the original vampire, blood and magic are the only cures for Lucifer. So, magical blood."

"Druid blood," Lire said. "Your blood, Frost."

Frost made a helpless gesture. "I don't think mine will be strong enough."

"No one is biting my mate." The roared words were every bit as furious as they should be. Gemini was Frost's other half. Biting was his right. No one else's.

Riku stared at him. There was nothing. No emotions. No thoughts. It was as if Frost had emptied him with the truth.

"There are other ways to get blood. We could do something like a transfusion. Like I said, I don't think I'm strong enough. But there's no reason we can't start with me, though. Just until we come up with a better choice." Frost opened his bag and pulled out an IV line and needle.

Lire shifted from foot to foot. "I maybe know of someone who could help, but I'll have to leave here, and there's no guarantee they'll agree. No one can hear my call from here. I'll have to go in person."

Frost didn't look his way. "Go. I'll be fine."

"Baby—"

"If he goes into a frenzy, no one here could protect you?" Lire said, cutting off Gemini.

"You couldn't either," Lucifer added, even though it was to his detriment.

Frost didn't stop working. "Lucifer won't hurt me."

"You're still the biggest idiot I know."

Frost met his stare. "You won't hurt me."

It hit Lucifer. Frost saw things no one else did. His calm wasn't a facade. He knew everything would be okay because he knew.

"Okay."

Gemini released a long tirade of cursing.

Lire leapt, vanishing through the mirror.

In no time, blood flowed from Frost to Lucifer. Gemini paced the floor. His hate-filled gaze never wavered from Lucifer. Riku walked away, disappearing into the next room. He still felt him.

Riku sat on the couch, but his mind was still a black void. Lucifer had to focus on something else. He chose Frost. Frost was the one who hurt the least.

"I can't believe you're doing this."

Frost chuckled. "Is it even helping?"

Lucifer turned inward. He could talk without feeling like there were razor blades in his throat, so there was that. "Yes, but you should stop."

"I will when Lire gets back."

Gemini released a low, deadly-sounding growl.

Lucifer ignored him, but they were on the same side. "It might be a long time before he returns. He might not come back. Lire is a traitor to his kind. He shouldn't be here."

"I'll remember that the next time your ass needs saving." Lire pounced from the mirror onto the bed beside him. He held up two bags of blood. "One wants me to tell you this isn't for you. It's to save the world."

Lucifer rolled his eyes. He hadn't asked anyone for help other than Frost. This place would freeze over before he did so again. Next time, he would let the world burn, especially since he had obviously lost his mate.

Frost grabbed both bags and hooked a line to each arm. "Normally, I would never do things this way, but it's you, so..."

Despite his situation, Lucifer laughed. The moment the first drop of fresh blood hit his veins, he recognized the connection. His nephew had helped. The other came from someone old and powerful, but he didn't know them. Druids didn't pass into Hell. They were reborn. They were all strangers to him.

Lire worked at Frost's side, helping him set up makeshift IV poles.

Lucifer studied him. He was one of Lucifer's favorite creations. His ability to destroy minds was... chef's kiss. Lucifer hated that Lire had turned on him.

"Why did you betray me?"

Lire didn't look his way, but a small smile touched his lips. "Only you would think of my going to protect your sister and her grandson as a betrayal."

"She turned on me first, so you speak on things you know nothing about."

Lire shook his head. He finally met Lucifer's stare. "Ultimately, it wasn't about her. I was given two mates."

Bitterness welled in Lucifer's throat. He couldn't offer that. That wasn't his place in the circle of life. The best he could give was a concubine of deviant demons. He couldn't compete with the power of soulmates. Lucifer had always been the disappointing twin. Of course, Celeste would use her powers to turn one of his favorites away from him. "That'll do it." He swallowed. "You all should go. I'll either live or I won't. You've done all you can." They had done more than they should or could by re-vealing his secrets and destroying his mating. He wasn't angry with them. Lucifer felt nothing. It was him. He had always been the abomination. Lire and Frost exchanged glances and then both found chairs to pull close to the bed. Gemini draped himself across Frost's feet with his gaze locked on the door. It was obvious he still expected an attack.

Lucifer was too tired to roll his eyes any-more today.

"How did Celeste betray you?"

Lire surprised Lucifer with the earnest-ness of his question. It genuinely sound-ed like he cared. That was... odd.

He supposed they had time to kill. Lu-cifer cleared his throat. "Despite us being identical, it was always obvious I was different. It was like I existed to be the dark to Celeste's light, but she was still the only person I loved. Obviously, we were close, so she knew from the very beginning about my curse. She kept it hidden. Protected me. Then I caught Jörmungandr's eye. I've always done as I pleased, and it pleased me to do him." An evil and dead-sounding chuckle escaped Lucifer. "I didn't take it seriously. We weren't mates. More than that, we were gods who could have and do whatever we wanted. It seemed so ridiculous to take our tryst to heart." Lucifer shifted uncomfortably. He couldn't sound weak, but the story was what it was. "In fact, there was a human with druid blood, who I enjoyed more than most. He fed me and kept my secret. There was no one else like me. Drinking blood to survive was unnatural in every way. As a druid, he saw the world differently. Blood is magic, and it made perfect sense to him that it would sustain me. After all, I was a god. He thought that's what we all do. Admittedly, I allowed him to hang on to that belief, but it didn't matter. There were no other gods that visited the plane Celeste had created. At least, that's what I thought." The rage still lived inside him and bubbled hot. Today, Lucifer didn't know if it was Riku's venom or the past that ate at his guts like acid.

"It seemed Jörmungandr thought we were more than I did. At some point, he followed me and learned everything. He struck up an affair with the druid to get even with me. That wasn't enough, though. He began to let it slip to others about my affliction. When I found out—" Lucifer swallowed. It had been the first time he had blacked out and leveled a town. He had torn them apart piece by piece, including his favorite lover. Lucifer didn't even recall doing it. He never did when the episodes hit.

"Let's just say I didn't handle it well. Celeste was furious and scared, but mostly just pissed. She banished me to this place and barred me from the heavens. Jörmungandr swore he would destroy me and level everything Celeste ever created for touching anyone else. Celeste is my sister. She should've had my back. I would've had hers. No matter what she did, I would've stood by her." He shrugged. Lucifer refused to show his pain over the loss of his only family so she could keep her toys. "So, I made this place my own. She isn't the only one who can create life. But I'm the dark one. Everything I make..." He motioned around him, knowing his creation would speak for itself. Maybe some of his demons had good hearts, but they were still poison.

Speaking of which. "Your mates. Are they human?"

Lire shook his head. "Vampire."

Still, Lire's touch would drive them insane. Celeste had created a race mirrored after him to protect her fragile beings from his creations. There was no way they had a good life together. Demons poisoned everything they touched. The venom literally secreted from their skin. The only way to stop it was at Lucifer's will.

"Come here."

To his credit, Lire didn't hesitate or question him. It was obvious he was a warrior. Lucifer understood why Celeste had chosen him.

When Lire was close enough to touch, Lucifer set his hand on his arm. "There. For your service today."

Lire blinked. "What did you do?"

"You're no longer a nope rope."

A laugh burst from Frost at the human joke about venomous snakes.

Lucifer realized he felt worlds better.

Lire still looked confused.

Lucifer sighed. "You can now touch people without infecting them."

He licked his lips, looking nervous. "Are you serious? I mean, I've been able to touch my mates for a while now, but no one else. Are you serious?"

Lucifer's attention was fully invested. The attack on his blood was all but forgotten. "How? How are you able to touch anyone?" If there was a loophole, Lucifer needed to know it.

Lire's expression snapped closed. "At great sacrifice to someone who didn't deserve it after years of torment at the hands of one of yours."

Tamil. That explained the lingering poison Lucifer had destroyed in his blood. It seemed he should make an effort to get to know this nephew. He had missed some things while dealing with his own drama. Lucifer felt better by the second now. He could take on anything. But bonding with a new to him family member had to wait. First, he had to save his relationship with Riku. That was one battle he already felt doomed to lose.

# Chapter Six

RIKU HADN'T GONE FAR. At first, he had simply moved to the couch in the sitting room and tried to deal. When he couldn't stand the sound of Brownie licking Yuri any longer—they sounded like they enjoyed the experience way too much—he moved to sit on the floor outside their bedroom door. He listened to Lucifer's story and the cadence of his voice. With every word, his chest hurt more. Lucifer had been Riku's creator's lover. Riku was a product of the hatred left over from infidelity. His entire purpose was to destroy Lucifer. He would never again get to sink his fangs into the man he loved, and his hopes of Lucifer ever loving him in return died a fiery death. It was no wonder Lucifer had resented their pairing. Why had Celeste done this cruel thing? He understood the banishment. The other gods would rip Lucifer to pieces for being an abomination. It was one thing for Celeste to create vampires for fun. Those were easily destroyed. Toys on a chessboard. But a vampire god? That was powerful and dangerous. Only his containment would appease them if they couldn't have his head. Of course, Celeste would do the only thing she could to save him, but why Riku?

Why would she pair Lucifer with the weapon created to destroy him? He didn't understand. However, he fully understood all the implications. They were doomed to half-lives. It was like they were meant to always have everything be just out of reach. Just like every time they had made love or been on the verge of it, something went wrong. Their problems always got in the way somehow. This would never be a proper union.

Riku didn't even feel the tears running down his face until Lucifer appeared and wiped them away. He plucked Riku from the floor and headed back to bed.

"Until you make your run for it, you'll still sleep with me."

Riku felt lifeless in Lucifer's arms as Lucifer tucked him into bed and then curled himself around him. His wings appeared. One draped over them.

"It's a real pain in the ass to always keep them put away."

"You shouldn't. I've always loved them." He stroked the feathers covering his body.

A soft moan escaped Lucifer. "Don't start something you don't intend to finish. I can take a lot of punishment, but we've been interrupted a lot lately."

Riku stroked the wing again. "Does that seriously turn you on?"

"Fuck." Lucifer dragged out the word, sounding on the edge of orgasm.

Riku risked a peek into his mind. A wave of lust nearly choked him. Disappointment hit Riku just as strongly. "I'm sorry you were cursed to a half-life with me. You'll never get to have that connection of me biting you, the way other mates have. Everything has just been so fucking unfair from day one with us. When I came here, I really thought everything would be okay."

Lucifer shoved his hand beneath Riku's shirt and rubbed his stomach. "Say you don't hate me, and everything will be okay."

That confused the fuck out of Riku. "Why would I hate you? You did nothing wrong. Not to me, anyhow."

"I didn't tell you about my curse. You didn't sign up for that."

"Neither of us signed up for anything. You didn't ask to be what you are. I didn't ask to be what I am. We didn't ask to be put together. I can never bite you." The defeat in Riku's voice echoed the pain in his soul. Mating was a very primal thing. This was forever, which was a damn long time when a person couldn't die. They would always be missing something.

"I would, though."

Riku blinked at Lucifer's random comment. "You would what?"

"I'd ask for you." Lucifer rolled, bringing Riku with him until Riku straddled his body. The move proved his energy level matched the exhaustion in his voice. He couldn't even be the one doing the holding. He wrapped his arms around Riku as Riku pressed his ear against Lucifer's chest.

Lucifer kept going. "If we were human, and just got to choose, I still would've crossed that club the other night. I still would've watched you all night and then shared every slow dance before going home with you. You'd never have peace with me stalking you. Nothing would be different about the way I feel."

Riku fought a fresh wave of tears. Lucifer didn't talk like this. He was more of an 'I'll see you dead before I see you with anyone else' type of guy. He didn't expect Lucifer to be soft. In his position, he couldn't be. Demons would tear him to shreds. But Riku was guilty of wanting a little softness just for him. He craved being special and seeing a side of Lucifer no one did. Instead, Frost got the sweet Lucifer. That hurt.

"To be fair, I call Frost an idiot pretty often." Riku cringed. Sometimes he forgot Lucifer heard his every thought. Still, Lucifer explained himself when he didn't have to. "But he chose to be my friend even knowing who I am. I suppose that's new for me. But I don't feel the same way about him as I do about you. You should know that. All you have to do is reach inside my head and take whatever you want. That's your right as my mate."

He liked to think Lucifer shut him out, so he didn't have to face the truth. Riku was scared of what he would find if he looked too closely at Lucifer's mind. He wasn't strong enough to feel the resentment of being paired with him. Riku had walked away from everything to come here. He couldn't look and see his sacrifice had been for nothing.

*Stop. What did you walk away from? Heaven? You were barred from that place because of me. Wulfe? It's cold there. Until recently, you kept yourself separate from the townspeople. Yuri? He's here and I doubt we'll be seeing the backside of him soon if Brownie gets his way. I know you chose a new plane—a deadly one—for me, but fuck. I love you. Are you telling me you lost more than you gained? If so, we're doomed.*

Riku went still inside at Lucifer's confession. Surely, he hadn't read those thoughts clearly. Taking risks always worked best with Lucifer. He would keep doing that. *You're right about Yuri. That's not what I meant. I love you with everything I have to give. Knowing I have to see and feel the disappointment in you every time we make love is killing me. You'll always be missing something with me. I can't feed you.* The confession fell before he even realized how he truly felt. If Lucifer needed blood, Riku wanted to provide it. He wanted to be all things to his mate, especially since Riku could never bite him.

Lucifer's hands ran down Riku's back before cupping his ass and squeezing. "I think you're forgetting that I drank your blood to claim you and nothing bad happened." *Not for that reason, anyhow.*

Riku's head shot up. His gaze moved over Lucifer's face. For the first time, he forced his way inside and saw that night through Lucifer's eyes. The vision of him covered in blood with no memory of what he had done hit him with enough power to steal his breath. Lucifer's pain was too much. Riku had to withdraw.

"I'm sorry." He swiped his lips across Lucifer's. "I'm so fucking sorry I couldn't see a path for us before Yuri made things sound so simple."

Lucifer held him away and stared at him at the confession. He felt Lucifer shifting through his memories. A smile exploded across his face as he brought the memory of Yuri fixing things to the forefront of Riku's brain. "That's it. My dog is getting a dog."

A laugh burst from Riku. It died as his clothes disappeared. Lucifer never had the patience to undress him properly.

He let it slide. Not only did he know Lucifer didn't feel well enough to expend that much energy, but he had fallen in love, knowing Lucifer had no patience. It was a hallmark of his personality.

Riku didn't have to undress Lucifer. He had never gotten dressed again after their disastrous last try. He wasn't useless, though. Lube appeared in his hand. He enjoyed watching the lust grow in Lucifer's eyes as he watched Riku oil his asshole. There were some benefits to taking a bit of extra time. Teasing could be fun. Riku didn't move fast. He slowly lowered himself onto Lucifer's waiting cock. Lucifer's aroused expression made the torture worthwhile. He felt the way Lucifer wanted to take control, but he barely had enough energy to stay conscious as it was. Only his desire to connect with his mate outweighed the heaviness of his eyelids. Riku felt all of that and took care of everything. He rocked on Lucifer's dick, tormenting himself. He stroked his erection while Lucifer watched. Riku gave him a show while taking the pleasure he wanted. His gums itched with the desire to bite and claim his rights, but that would never be. He had to let that go. Some of his mate was better than none. Riku would take this over anything with anyone else.

"Come here." Lucifer towed Riku closer. His fingernail grew into a claw, and he sliced his neck. "Fix it. You don't have to bite." His voice turned seductive, luring Riku the way he did souls to their doom. Riku knew that and didn't care. Lucifer was right. There were ways around biting. His gums still ached, but the moment Lucifer's blood filled his mouth, Riku forgot everything. An orgasm exploded through him, coming from his spirit. He shook as he feared for his sanity and then Lucifer bit him. Riku heard colors. He saw sound. It was euphoric and what he imagined felt like an LSD trip. He floated in the clouds as his body jerked with ecstasy. Riku didn't miss the sounds Lucifer made or the way he pumped Riku full of cum. He didn't miss a thing. Riku had never been more connected in his life.

*I love you, my mate. This is no half-life.*

As the words brushed his brain, tears filled Riku's eyes. He was right. This wasn't half of anything. It was

whole–ass perfection. Riku would trea-
sure this for eternity.

Lucifer had no idea how long he slept.
That was not something he usually
did. His body needed repair. The house
seemed unusually quiet as he padded
his way into the sitting room. Riku
sat reading with two heads on his lap.
He took turns mindlessly petting the

two. The contentment filled the air with peace.

Riku glanced up as he entered the room. "Hey. You're back to full strength."

Brownie immediately leaped from the couch and went on alert as if expecting admonishment for being lazy.

Lucifer didn't correct the behavior. In the world of hellhounds, softness got a doggie killed. While Brownie was mostly protected by his position, others would still push him, trying to take his spot. Truthfully, he was irreplaceable. He wasn't Lucifer's guard. Lucifer didn't need a guard. He was Lucifer's fur baby. Of course, he would eat nails before he admitted that.

Riku's smile said he read Lucifer's thoughts.

Lucifer had to move along. He filled the spot Brownie vacated. "What are you reading?"

"Smut." Riku smiled unrepentantly. "It's highly unrealistic. I love it."

Lucifer chuckled at the happiness in Riku's voice. It was the first time he had felt normal in... he had no idea. Time had stopped having any meaning forever ago. It seemed so strange for this to be the life he wanted, but it was. Just his man and two dogs with nothing to do but whatever they chose. A family. His throat swelled. He had to go to the torture room and remind himself of his position. Lucifer couldn't start thinking about Celeste doing this for him. It was so much easier to hate her.

"I have to check on things and make sure no one is getting ideas about over-throwing me. One day out of sight is out of mind for these fuckers."

Riku smiled. "Okay." He sounded un-bothered.

Lucifer poked at Riku's brain. To his shock, Riku truly was fine with whatev-er Lucifer needed to do to keep this mess under control. He saw Lucifer's posi-tion as just that—his place in the uni-verse. Beyond that, Riku saw himself as Lucifer's peace. That was his place, and he wanted it. He blew Lucifer away. Lucifer stole a kiss. He took his time, making sure Riku missed him. Lucifer forced himself to stop before he chose to stay. An uprising would take way more time than a simple torture session. He had to get to work.

Lucifer stood. "Tell your friend goodbye, Brownie. It's time to go to work."

*Lucifer!* The panicked scream tore through his mind. His gaze shot to Riku. Riku shot to his feet, as if he heard it too.

"Frost."

They raced to the bedroom. As they reached the bed, he grabbed Riku around the waist. His wings expanded as he shot through the mirror. He glanced back to see Brownie giving Yuri a leg up before leaping through behind him. While Lucifer could zap wherever he wanted, he hadn't given Riku that ability yet and he wouldn't for anyone else. Not even Brownie. The more beings that could freely come and go in Hell, the more weaknesses there were to exploit. Outside the mirror, Riku and Lucifer each snagged a dog and followed the lingering wisps of Frost's panic to his location with a single thought. They found themselves at Riku's house. Gemini danced above the magic fire, inches from being roasted and held by invisible strings. Frost stood by helplessly.

The power that pulsed in the air was nearly enough to bring him to his knees. At the first glimpse of Jörmungandr, Lucifer waved his arm, sending Riku, Brownie, Yuri, Gemini, and Frost away. The moment he felt them land safely on his bed, he sealed the mirror, trapping them out of Jörmungandr's reach.

A smile exploded across Jörmungandr's face. A beautiful laugh—a laugh of the heavens—poured from Jörmungandr. His sky-blue eyes danced with humor. "Do you intend to send this entire town to Hell to keep them from me? What about this whole dumb little planet?"

"If I have to, yes."

Jörmungandr cocked his head to one side and studied Lucifer. "Oh, good. I've left this alone long enough for you to care about something. That'll make it so much more fun to destroy this useless place." Despite his light blond hair and flawless beauty, he definitely had an evil streak. Lucifer wondered if he wouldn't have been a better choice to lead Hell. Of course, most of the worst things in Hell had been created by Lucifer, so probably not.

"I don't give a shit if you destroy this place, as stupid as that would be on your part. This planet means nothing to me. But it means everything to Celeste. It's her favorite toy."

Irritation flashed in Jörmungandr's eyes. "Still? Ridiculous. She's like a child with her dolls. Very well. I'll have to settle with breaking you." In a flash, Jörmungandr was inches from him. Before he made contact, he bounced backward off the very wide chest of Odin.

Lucifer didn't have time to recover from that shock before he got another. Soft fingers entwined with his. He found Celeste at his side. She didn't look his way.

Her spine was like steel, but she held his hand. He felt her love.

"This has nothing to do with you, Odin. Go back to your low-key alcoholism and leave the trash to me."

Odin snorted. "This has everything to do with me. Although I know she's more than capable of handling you, what kind of man would I be if I let my woman fight this battle?"

Lucifer's eyebrows shot up.

A wicked smile stretched Celeste's lips.

It was true.

"Odin?" he mouthed.

Her smile grew and her eyes danced with happiness. Well, he couldn't argue with that.

"Step aside. Lucifer is mine. He's always been mine." The way he said 'mine' sounded so sickening, it made Lucifer's stomach churn.

Lucifer rolled his eyes. This whole thing was about Jörmungandr's hurt pride. He was the original grudge holder.

An evil chuckle fell from Lucifer's lips, mocking Jörmungandr. Jörmungandr didn't stand a chance against the three of them, and he knew it. "How embarrassing for you, Monnie. Why aren't you humiliated for throwing a fit over getting dicked down? My plane would freeze before I ever admitted anyone was so good in bed, they had me destroying worlds."

Hatred already flashed in Jörmungandr's eyes. It doubled when Odin laughed at the taunt. "You'd know all about de-stroying things in temper tantrums, wouldn't you? Isn't that exactly how you ended up banished?"

Lucifer shrugged. "I'd still be cozy in my fiery, hot bog if you hadn't stormed your ass down here. I've accepted my fate. You should do the same and move along. There's nothing for you here."

"Nah. I think I'll stay. My toy made a little house and a cozy fire here. I can chill until I've snatched him away from you and crushed his tiny skull. Maybe I'll entertain myself by roasting a few townsfolk in the meantime. The quicker you let me have my way, the fewer people that'll get hurt."

Ugh. Lucifer really wanted to choke the life from him.

"I seriously doubt you want to feel my wrath, Monnie." It was the first time he had heard Celeste's voice in ages. He fought the way the sound made his eyes sting. "Everything here is mine. A single hair out of place will have you hanging by your entrails in my study for the rest of eternity. This isn't a war you want. When my brother was banished, our deal was met. You're the one breaking those terms." She ran her hand down Odin's spine. "We will see that contract honored."

Odin glanced over his shoulder and smiled.

Damn. They were in love. He would not have seen that coming in a million years. He hoped the union endured. Otherwise, this world would see a vampire–werewolf war like none other. Lucifer would likely be forced to unleash a demon army.

Jörmungandr ran his tongue over his teeth, obviously doing his best to hold back the rage. "I'll see my creation returned, then."

"Over my dead body."

Celeste squeezed his hand at Lucifer's growled words. "Riku's soul has been bound to Lucifer. He's no longer yours."

An evil–looking smile stretched Jörmungandr's lips. "Is that how we're playing this?" He disappeared and reappeared almost instantly. Fen, a Scottish vampire who had been sent to protect Frost, hung from his hand like a rag doll. "Then I think I'll take this one." He was gone again before anyone could protest. Not that Lucifer cared, as long as he was gone.

Celeste pinched the spot between her eyes. She dropped her hand, looking tired. "One battle at a time, I suppose. I doubt he's dumb enough to harm him."

"You look beautiful." He didn't mean to say it. The power of seeing his twin again was too much. He couldn't think straight.

A sad smile touched her lips. "Vain, as always. You know it's like looking in a mirror."

A bark of laughter burst from Lucifer. It was the most Celeste response he had ever heard.

"I miss you."

Her confession had the laughter dying in his throat. She didn't stop.

"I know you can't see it. It's easier to hate me. But I've always done everything I can to protect you. You can't know the relief I felt when I realized Riku is your other half."

There she went. Celeste always claimed the knowledge just came to her—like visions. Her pairings weren't always strategic. Personally, he thought she was just so damn good at her job that it was mostly subconscious now. She cast a loving glance Odin's way. "You know me, I just know."

Lucifer nearly sighed in relief. It seemed Odin was hers. After all these lifetimes, a god pairing had revealed itself. They wouldn't be destroying worlds.

Her shoulders squared. "I can't stay, but I'm kind of glad for Jörmungandr's tantrum over your mating. It let me see you. I still don't know how he found out about you claiming Riku, but he likely had some system for when his weapon was engaged." She smiled. "I knew Frost would save you."

Fuck. She really did always have a plan that was a hundred steps ahead of everyone else, even for the brother she knew was a monster.

Celeste kissed his cheek. "I love you."

She didn't wait for a response. Her fingers linked with Odin's and she was gone.

Lucifer stared at nothing, trying his damnedest to feel nothing. "I love you too." His chest hurt. It felt like he was dying. It took him a second to realize it was because he had sealed Riku in Hell. His other half was behind a veil. That was the pain he felt. That was what he had to tell himself. It was time to leave this place behind and let Celeste handle her realm. Lucifer was tired. He just wanted back the normal Riku had brought into his life.

# Chapter Seven

THE RAGE WAS MASSIVE. His fear was even bigger. Riku was the only thing that could kill Lucifer, and he just might. No matter how hard they pushed against the mirror, it wouldn't budge. When they finally gave up, they all stood with their hands on their hips looking equal amounts of angry. It was possibly for different reasons, though. Riku couldn't imagine Frost, Gemini, or Yuri were too happy about finding themselves trapped in Hell.

"This used to be a quiet town. There weren't any gods showing up, dangling people over fires."

At Gemini's enraged words, Frost's shoulders fell. "I know. Your life was fine before me. I'm sorry."

Gemini growled. It sounded very large cat-like. "It isn't you. You're the only reason I stay. You didn't choose this healer position."

Riku couldn't breathe. Truth be told, he was the reason they were here. He could have chosen any town to rest. Riku could have kept his distance from the people. Everything he did felt like one big fuck-up. He'd put these people in danger.

Lucifer's arms encircled him from behind. No one noticed. They were too busy staring at the mirror. Riku didn't startle. He had smelled him the moment he appeared. His heart had known its other half had arrived.

Frost spun, as if he too felt Lucifer's presence. He opened his mouth, as if to blast him.

Brownie beat him to the punch. He turned human. "How fucking dare you lock me away? It's my job to protect you. You insult my abilities. It's my job," he repeated, sounding like the demon dog he was.

Lucifer didn't feel guilty. It was all there in his mind. He had known none of them stood a chance against a god.

Still, he placated him. "I needed you here to protect my mate. He's my weak spot and my enemies will always know it. You did your job. You protected my back."

Brownie sniffed. He seemed somewhat appeased. "Okay. I know you didn't have time to say that. He's too important."

Riku bit back a smile. Now wasn't the time.

Thankfully, Lucifer kept the focus on himself. "You should be safe to go home now. Celeste took care of things. You're, unfortunately, down a guard now, Frost. But I'm sure my sister will have him back in no time... hopefully in one piece."

"What? Who?"

"Fen."

"Oh." Frost didn't look as upset as Riku would've thought. Then he remembered Fen had been one of the vampires that had been used against Wulfe's pack leader when his relationship went south. Riku would keep it to himself that he had been the one to suggest Audor take Fen on a date. Oops. He genuinely hoped the guy was okay. Riku felt certain Jörmungandr wouldn't challenge Celeste by actually killing one of her creations. He was childish and spoiled, but he wasn't stupid.

Frost made a helpless motion. "Thank you for coming when I called. I wasn't sure if you'd hear me, but I didn't know what else to do."

Lucifer's affection for Frost rolled off him in waves. Riku tried not to be jealous. Lucifer deserved at least one real friend. He had been denied that for too long.

"Of course. I'll always come when you call. Don't let that get you killed."

Frost ran his hand down Gemini's arm. "It's not me I'm worried about. I don't know why he chose to torture Gemini instead of me, but I can't have that. My heart can't take it."

Gemini wrapped his arms around Frost and kissed his temple. "I'm okay, baby. Luckily, I didn't lose any fur the way Yuri did."

*I'm perfectly fine with the way that worked out.*

A huge smile spread across Riku's lips as Yuri's words brushed his mind.

Brownie flashed a smile Yuri's way too, as if he heard.

"We should head home. Our house is a mess from our intruder. I'm glad everyone is okay." He hesitated. "Except Fen, of course. Hopefully, that works out."

To be fair, Jörmungandr was a god. There really wasn't anything they could do. Frost wasn't being heartless. He just put his faith in Celeste, as he should.

"A leg up, Brownie."

At Lucifer's command, Brownie turned back into a hellhound and let the pair use his back to climb through the mirror.

*I should probably go help.* Yuri sounded like he didn't really want to go, but he felt obligated. Frost had done his best to heal his burns.

"I think you should stay. Frost and Gemini probably need some time alone."

*Okay. That's true.* His chipper tone died a swift death. *What about the house, though? It's my duty to protect it. Is it okay after Jörmungandr got ahold of it?*

Lucifer didn't respond.

Riku looked his way, expecting he would answer. He merely looked as if he waited for Riku to finish his conversation.

"Oh no. That's a bad sign. Did he level the house?"

Lucifer blinked. "Why did you ask like that? I'm not keeping anything from you. It looked okay from the outside. I don't know about the inside."

A thought occurred to him. "Can you not hear Yuri in this form?"

Lucifer shook his head. "He isn't my companion. He's yours. I can only hear Brownie. That's how it works."

*Wait. What?* Yuri sounded as confused as Riku felt.

"What do you mean? Are you saying he's like my pet?"

*Hey, now. I'm no one's pet. I love you and all, but I'm a free wolf.*

Riku couldn't blame Yuri for his outage. "I love you too. Don't worry about my feelings. I'd feel the same in your place."

Lucifer and Brownie exchanged glances. It wasn't really fair for them to think of him as ignorant. Wolves were Odin's creation. Riku didn't get in Odin's business. Lucifer took on an exaggerated, patient expression. "Yuri saved your life. At least, that was his full intent. He truly believed you were in danger when he leapt into that fire. He's a creation of Odin. That type of act always comes with a high reward. In Yuri's case, he's been promoted to a guardian wolf. Your guardian."

*Whoa. Really? Odin sees me? Me? I'm no one. Is that how you became a guard?* Yuri asked, focusing on Brownie.

*Oh.*

At Yuri's 'oh,' Riku realized Brownie had answered, but Riku couldn't hear.

*He says—again—he's not a creation of Odin. He earned his position through violence and blood.*

Lucifer didn't roll his eyes, but Riku felt it. *It wasn't quite that dramatic, but I'll let him keep his pride.*

At Lucifer's words, Riku realized he could tell when Lucifer kept his thoughts between them. It was nice having a private line.

*I thought you couldn't hear Yuri.*

*I didn't. I heard Brownie's answer. He's named Brownie, for fuck's sake.*

Riku turned his head so Brownie wouldn't see the way he fought not to laugh.

*Don't get me wrong, he's pretty badass, but he has a very soft and gooey center—like a Brownie. He'll be a good mate to Yuri.*

Riku's eyebrows tried crawling into his hairline. *They're mates?*

*Of course, they can speak just like us. Brownie is an alpha. He can speak telepathically to any lesser animal, but Yuri isn't my creation, and Yuri isn't lesser. If anything, a guardian wolf is the highest a wolf can hope to climb, especially guardian to a godling. If it makes you feel better, neither of them realizes it either. I'm kind of looking forward to watching the drama unfold.*

Riku shook his head. He waved away the hounds. "You two should go do something. I want to check my man for injuries."

*He never touched me,* Lucifer reminded him.

"Don't ruin my fun."

*I should check on the house.*

"Yuri wants to check on the house. Is it okay if Brownie gives him a leg up?"

Lucifer made a shooing motion. "Go with him. Keep him safe. A guardian wolf is a high prize for anyone looking to lash out at us."

Riku focused on Yuri. *He knows you can take care of yourself. He's just getting*

*Brownie out of the house so we can be as loud as we want.*

*Ew.*

Riku laughed as Yuri used Brownie's back to leap through the mirror. Brownie followed without looking back.

Riku focused on Lucifer the second they were alone. "Tell me what happened. Every detail. I was cut off from you, which better never happen again. It felt like you'd died."

A sexy smile touched Lucifer's lips. "I appreciate you waiting until we're alone to scold me." He swept Riku from his feet. "You can wait a little longer for answers."

Riku wanted to be aggravated, but it was impossible in Lucifer's arms. This was his mate. They were together. Literally, nothing else mattered.

While Lucifer knew Riku deserved answers, he couldn't deal right now. He felt too raw from seeing his sister and it was exhausting trying to keep that from Riku. Every day, it got a little harder to keep Riku from penetrating deeper and deeper into his mind. Soon there would be nowhere he could hide.

"Oh, baby. It's okay to totally understand her reasoning and still feel bitter. You can love her and still feel hurt over her decisions. It's completely valid to feel torn."

Well, shit. It didn't seem he hid as well as he thought. He shook his head as he settled on the bed with his back against the headboard and Riku across his lap. "You do realize I'm still Lucifer, right? I'm still the same evil, dangerous, and powerful god I was before we met. I'm still undesirable number one—the great deceiver. Whatever else people say. It's all valid. Just because that doesn't extend to you doesn't mean anything has changed. When you were constantly rejecting me, I could've killed you. I wanted to most days."

Riku didn't seem bothered. "I'm aware. You are all those things, and someone has to be. There'll never be a light without a dark. Your sister and you are the most powerful beings in existence. One of you had to be the counterbalance. One cannot exist without the other to keep things in check. That's just the way the universe works. But that doesn't mean you should be denied this." He ran his hand up Lucifer's chest. His shirt disappeared beneath Riku's touch. "You can do everything necessary to be who you are and still have a life that's only for you."

He was right. There was nothing that said he couldn't have a mate he loved, guardian pets and a couple of friends. Nowhere was that written. He had never followed the rules. This was no different. In fact, this was exactly the counterbalance he needed. He was long overdue to have someone to keep his temper in check, so he didn't fall into blackouts that destroyed entire cities.

"I know you didn't choose this, but I also know you're strong enough to have not chosen me. You could've stayed away forever, but you didn't. You're just stubborn enough to have done it. What's wrong with you?"

A laugh burst from Riku, just as he hoped. "Maybe I'm touched in the head. Maybe that's why Celeste chose me." He shifted positions and straddled Lucifer. "Or maybe I'm just so fucking infatuated that I'll overlook anything as long as I can do this." He swiped a sweet kiss across Lucifer's lips.

Personally, Lucifer hoped it was that one. He could handle being the center of Riku's obsession.

Riku leaned back and peeled off his shirt. His gaze locked on the ceiling. "No one is dropping through this thing while we're enjoying our day, are they?"

Lucifer laughed. He didn't mind an audience, but—in this case—they wouldn't get one. "No one can come through without my permission or a key. There's only one key, and it's a living, breathing person and a highly guarded secret."

"Why is the entrance above your bed?"

Lucifer rolled, pinning Riku beneath him. "So I can keep an eye on it. Do you want to keep asking questions, or can I fuck you now?"

"The second one, please."

As always, Lucifer didn't have the patience to undress. In the blink of an eye, they were nude, with Riku lubed to perfection. "I swear you'll get foreplay and all that one of these days. Right now, my restraint is nonexistent." He impaled Riku. Lucifer groaned as Riku's body welcomed him. "I have to have this." Riku's body filled a hole in his chest. This wasn't sex. He connected with the other half of his soul, and he needed that. It was vital he touched that love he had been denied. It was beautiful. But Lucifer planned to fuck him like it was ugly and he hated him because he needed to mark his territory. He needed Riku to know no one else could do for him what Lucifer did.

Lucifer held Riku at the perfect angle and sawed in and out of him, hitting exactly where Riku needed until all he could do was cling to the headboard and try to suck air. He fed on the sounds Riku made. Lucifer was temptation. He could and would addict Riku to his touch until he overlooked anything and there was a lot he would have to overlook.

Riku's gaze collided with his. Fire danced in his eyes. "I'll not be overlooking you touching anyone else. You'll wish I had actually killed you, and I still can."

Damn. He needed to mind his thoughts. "You know better. Nothing compares to a mate. You're entirely too coherent."

"Me?" Riku released a loud moan, obviously trying to cling to his thoughts. "You're the one having whole conversations. Fuck, Lucifer. Don't stop."

Lucifer took the plea to heart. He didn't stop even after he dragged out a powerful orgasm where he felt every second, and he didn't stop after the second. Lucifer had no plans to take mercy on his sexy man. His black soul needed its fill.

The outside of the house seemed un-touched, just as Lucifer said. At the door, Yuri turned human and let them in-side. Brownie followed suit, but he near-ly tripped over his tongue in the process. While he obviously found the wolf irre-sistible, that was all based on his per-sonality. He wasn't one to care all that much about looks. After all, he certainly was no visual prize, but goddamn. He had not been prepared. Not by a long shot.

"Damn. I forgot to clean up. My hand hurt too badly to wash dishes before I went to Frost's place. Then you showed up, and I got sidetracked."

Brownie did not hear a word. He was just red hair and a solid body. Brownie knew Yuri was the son of a now dead alpha, but he didn't know what he expected. He was big enough to be an alpha himself and just fucking beautiful. Brownie didn't totally understand the way he felt.

Whiskey-colored eyes focused on him. "If you don't mind, I'll just wash these dishes before we go back. I don't know what my living situation will look like from now on, but I know I can't leave all this out to rot."

"It's fine. You have time. I'll check the perimeter and make one hundred percent sure that everything is safe." He had to walk away before he embarrassed himself. While Brownie knew Yuri had enjoyed the way he made his fur all fluffy and clean, that wasn't the same as being seen with a guy like him.

They definitely didn't match. Yuri was beautiful.

Outside, he turned hellhound and made a quick trip around the outside of the house, sniffing for any sign of trouble. Then he froze and waited. He felt her before she appeared.

Celeste always looked beautiful. She was the heavenly blonde and blue-eyed dream of the gods. A white gown flowed down her body, highlighting her every perfection. Her eyes looked sad today.

"How is he?"

Brownie turned human. "He's okay. It was obvious he was trying to hide his feelings, but Riku is making him better."

She nodded. "Thank you for keeping an eye on him. I worried how things would go once Riku moved into his plane where I can't see. In his core, I know my brother is good, but I wasn't sure if he would see Riku as a weakness or a blessing."

"It's a little of both, I think. He keeps ordering me to watch his mate or his mate's guardian wolf."

Celeste's eyes sparkled with humor, but she kept her thoughts to herself. "Yeah. My love definitely did me a solid by giving Yuri the honor he deserves, despite it tying him to Hell."

Brownie dipped his chin. "I hear love is wild like that." He would never know. His path was to serve. It was an honor to have climbed so high, no matter how hard he had struggled for it.

Celeste cupped his face and kissed his forehead. "I swear you'll be rewarded in ways you've never dreamed of for keeping my twin safe and being my eyes where I can't go. You'll see."

It was already a blessing beyond words to be so honored by a goddess. Not just any goddess, but *the* goddess. He couldn't ask for more.

"Go. Enjoy your day with your new friend. He needs you, likely even more than you need him."

Brownie couldn't imagine that, but he wouldn't argue with being ordered to spend time with Yuri. Celeste disappeared as easily as she appeared. Brownie made his way back inside. Yuri stood at the kitchen sink fully dressed, to Brownie's dismay. Still, he was flawless. Brownie couldn't think of a single reason for Yuri to need him at all, but he would stick by the pup. There was just something about him. Brownie would figure it out.

Gemini tossed things in a trash bag. When he found the glass figurine his mother had given him for protection, he sighed in relief to see it was still in one piece. He placed it back on the corner shelf where it belonged. When the whirlwind had landed inside their home, bringing the cold scent of sea water, Gemini's confusion had slowed his reaction time. He couldn't stop thinking about that. When tested, Gemini couldn't protect his mate. Frost had been forced to call out for another man. Granted, that was exactly what their terrorizer wanted. That was the entire reason Gemini was being roasted, but still. While Gemini was beyond grateful for the love he had been handed, he didn't understand why Celeste had chosen him. It was obvious he wasn't strong enough for this role. Even now, after the day they'd had, Frost still treated a patient as if unmoved, while Gemini was at home—alone—having an existential crisis.

"You were chosen long before you were born. That's why your mother had spells drawn all over your body. It was to protect you today. Any other being would've burned alive before my brother reached you."

Gemini patted his chest at the sudden arrival of the golden goddess in his living room. Before Frost, he might have crawled across glass to meet such a flawless woman. Now he was simply awed by the glow of her skin.

"It's Celeste," she said, clearing up things a hair.

He shuffled from foot to foot. "Am I supposed to bow or anything? This is new territory."

A beautiful chuckle filled the air. "No, dear. You don't owe me a thing. I'm very grateful for the way you protect my healer. He saved my brother. You can't know what that means to me. It's what he was created to do. A future seen too long ago to recount. But it took a billion tiny choices and actions to end up exactly where he needed to be. Without you, he wouldn't understand the love it took for such an act, saving the life of the dark one. Your love—so flawless and unending—makes him see the best in others. It makes him want the best for everyone, so they too might live to have what he does." Her voice turned sad. "He lives in constant guilt, thinking about how he fails you. Frost sees the way others get to spend their lives fully invested in their other halves and he aches for what he steals from you. He doesn't need a powerful man who rushes in to save the day. Frost needs a love that doesn't quit on him or hate him when he feels like he does nothing but let you down. Your role is so much bigger and more important than what you can see. But I *can* see it and I need you to stop doubting my choices because this position is killing him all because he thinks it's costing him you."

Gemini rubbed his forehead. Frost couldn't lose him, but he saw why he felt that way. It was Gemini's fault. He fought so hard to be everything that he was actually doing nothing to ease Frost's burden. Frost always fought like hell for them. He always ran on empty to make sure Gemini felt seen too.

He dropped his hand, intent on swearing he would find a way to fix things. Celeste vanished. The front door opened, and Frost walked inside.

Gemini sat his trash bag aside and moved to greet Frost. "Hey, baby." He swept Frost off his feet. "Come on. You can slobber cry all over me as you tell me all about this latest Were pregnancy loss. I've got you."

He wasn't the least bit surprised when Frost's first tear fell. Celeste was right. Frost needed him, but not to physically save him. He craved a lifeline to cling to in the exhaustion he had been dropped into. Gemini could do that. He could do anything. As long as he got to hold Frost, he would be whatever his mate called upon him to be. It was love.

# Chapter Eight

ADMITTEDLY, RIKU HAD BEEN a little scared to explore past the bedroom and sitting room of his new home. He hadn't been sure where he was allowed or what he would find. After a couple of weeks of being nosey, he realized the place had some sort of glamor cast over it. At first, he thought Lucifer was just zapping to wherever he went sometimes because he didn't want to believe his eyes, but no. Lucifer walked through walls. Once he realized certain door-ways were simply hidden, and Lucifer was the only one who could see them, he felt a little ridiculous. Unfortunately, he regretted asking about it the moment he learned the doorways led to places he shouldn't be... nor did he want to go. The rest of the home looked like the old castle it was, except with all the modern updates and everything was gold. Riku loved it. I reminded him of his favorite times throughout history.

He didn't get as bored as he feared. With Yuri and Brownie at his side, Riku still saw his friends and went to Frost's barbecues. That was as far as he strayed from the mirror. He was more than a little surprised that no one eyed him with hatred. They also accepted Brownie with an ease only their community could. They were a ragtag bunch, after all. Mostly, Riku just found ways to entertain himself when Lucifer was busy.

He read and played games with his dog-gy companions. It was a peaceful existence he never could have pictured for his future after learning how it would be spent. He had never been happier... or more in love.

Riku found Yuri asleep on the couch. It had been this way for weeks. Occasionally, he checked on the house with Brownie, but he was always back. Someone had lovingly covered him with a blanket. It was sweet watching the way Brownie cared for him, but also a little heartbreaking. It was obvious Brownie didn't see himself as good enough for Yuri. Meanwhile, Yuri had been rejected so harshly over the years and made so many bad choices, he feared making any move at all. Riku couldn't fix it.

He squeezed into the only empty spot on the couch and ran his fingers through Yuri's fur. Yuri was so fluffy. He had never seen a wolf so well groomed. Riku shook his head. He didn't know how two hounds could be so blind.

Yuri yawned and stretched as he turned human. "Hey."

Riku smiled. "Hey. Aren't you uncomfortable always sleeping on the couch?"

Yuri shrugged. "Anything indoors is better than how I lived before you took me in."

"Maybe you should just live here."

Yuri looked uncomfortable. His gaze slid away. He felt the way Yuri wanted to say yes, but he had promised to keep the house safe, and he didn't want to disappoint Riku. "What about the house?"

It was Riku's turn to shrug. "We can keep doing what we've been doing or put it up for sale—you keep the money, of course."

"I don't know." The discomfort practically rolled off him in waves. Riku felt the way he was scared to make a move and ruin his life again.

"How about we at least have you pick out a bedroom here? That way, you can have your own bed. You can decorate it however you like. Lucifer and I can conjure you anything you want. Then you could just figure things out later."

Yuri took a moment before answering. "Yeah. Okay."

Riku stood, and Yuri followed. He conjured Yuri some clothes. Riku didn't really care, but it made everyone else more comfortable. After touring a few rooms, without much enthusiasm from Yuri, Riku had an idea. He led Yuri to a bedroom across the hall from Brownie's room. That had Yuri letting his insecurities go. He wanted to be closer to Brownie.

As if feeling Yuri's presence, Brownie practically ripped open his door. The moment he set eyes on Yuri, he softened. "Hey. You're up."

Riku hid a smile. Brownie was human and dressed. He looked like he belonged in a biker gang, which fit. The style definitely matched his scars.

Yuri immediately turned twice as bright. "Hey! Guess what? Riku gave me this bedroom. He says I can decorate it however I want."

It got even harder to hide his humor. Apparently, Yuri had chosen his room, for sure.

"What do you think I should do in here? I don't know shit about decorating anything."

Brownie crossed the hall and joined Yuri. Riku silently backed out and left them alone. He smiled all the way back to the living room. Lucifer sat, waiting.

"Are you meddling?"

A laugh burst from Riku. "No. Just finding Yuri a more comfortable place to sleep."

"Mhmm." Lucifer didn't sound like he believed it, but then again, he could read Riku's mind. It wasn't like he could lie or hide anything from his other half. "Since you have them occupied." Lucifer patted his knee. "You should sit on my lap."

The evil glint in Lucifer's eye had a wave of lust rising inside him. Goddess, he loved this bad boy, kinky dream man he'd been given. Riku couldn't get enough. Still, he played coy. He couldn't be too easy all the time. "I don't know. What'll you give me if I do?"

A ring appeared between Lucifer's fingers. "Maybe I can lure you in with a wedding ring? You don't have one yet."

Riku took a step closer. The piece was black with inset red rubies. Gorgeous.

"That is pretty. I like the way it shimmers." He still didn't give in, though.

A book appeared in Lucifer's other hand. "Then maybe this."

"Shut up." Riku rushed across the room and crawled onto Lucifer's lap. He eyed the book. "I didn't even know a new one in the series had released."

A sexy laugh rumbled from Lucifer. "That's why you have me. Your pleasure is always mine." His voice was pure temptation, luring Riku to his wildest dreams.

Riku met Lucifer's stare. He knew he had to look as dewy-eyed as he felt. Adoration filled him to overflowing. To be known and loved the way Lucifer knew and loved him was priceless. "Thank you." He settled against Lucifer's chest. After putting on the ring, he gently tugged one of Lucifer's wings to cover him—like settling in with a blanket. Riku rubbed the feathers. "Tell me about your day."

"Tease."

Riku forced his hands still. He always forgot how hot playing with Lucifer's wings made him. "Sorry. Go ahead."

Lucifer kissed his head. "No. No apologies. I want your touch."

Riku's eyes fell closed. He took a deep breath. The smell of marshmallows cooking over a campfire filled his nose. There was no way he could have known that his heaven existed in Hell. Every day, he prayed for more, even though his prayers weren't heard here.

"I hear your prayers."

Riku's throat swelled at the whispered words. Sometimes, emotions choked him when he least expected it. He had spent so long fighting the biggest blessing he ever received, he didn't always know how to handle the enormity of it. Never again. Riku had found his home. He wouldn't budge.

Keep an eye out for the next Devilish, *Unguarded*.

# About the Author

CHARITY PARKERSON IS AN award-winning and multi-published author with several companies. Born with no filter from her brain to her mouth, she decided to take this odd quirk and insert it in her characters. One of her greatest loves is writing morally gray characters. You'll find them scattered throughout her hundreds of titles.

*Nine-time Readers' Favorite Award Winner

*2015 Passionate Plume Award Finalist

*2013 Reviewers' Choice Award Winner

*2012 ARRA Finalist for Favorite Paranormal Romance

*Five-time winner of The Mistress of the Darkpath

Connect with her online:

*Sign up for her newsletter: https://bit.ly/charityparkersonnewsletter

*Join her readers' group on Facebook: http://bit.ly/CharitysTribe

*Website: https://www.charityparkerson.com

*A list of her social media accounts and giveaways all in one place: http://hy.page/charityparkerson